The Savage Life 3

Lock Down Publications and
Ca$h Presents
The Savage Life 3
A Novel by **J-Blunt**

The Savage Life 3

Lock Down Publications
P.O. Box 870494
Mesquite, Tx 75187

Visit our website
www.lockdownpublications.com

Copyright 2020 by J-Blunt
The Savage Life 3

All rights reserved. No part of this book may be reproduced in any form or by electronic or mechanical means, including information storage and retrieval systems without permission in writing from the publisher, except by a reviewer who may quote brief passages in review.
First Edition February 2020
Printed in the United States of America

This is a work of fiction. Names, characters, places, and incidents either are products of the author's imagination or are used fictitiously. Any similarity to actual events or locales or persons, living or dead, is entirely coincidental.

Lock Down Publications
Like our page on Facebook: Lock Down Publications @
www.facebook.com/lockdownpublications.ldp
Cover design and layout by: **Dynasty Cover Me**
Book interior design by: **Shawn Walker**
Edited by: **Lauren Burton**

3

Stay Connected with Us!

Text **LOCKDOWN** to 22828 to stay up-to-date with new releases, sneak peeks, contests and more…

Submission Guideline.

Submit the first three chapters of your completed manuscript to ldpsubmissions@gmail.com, subject line: Your book's title. The manuscript must be in a .doc file and sent as an attachment. The document should be in Times New Roman, double-spaced and in size 12 font. Also, provide your synopsis and full contact information. If sending multiple submissions, they must each be in a separate email.

Have a story but no way to send it electronically? You can still submit to LDP/Ca$h Presents. Send in the first three chapters, written or typed, of your completed manuscript to:

LDP: Submissions Dept
Po Box 870494
Mesquite, Tx 75187

DO NOT send original manuscript. Must be a duplicate.

Provide your synopsis and a cover letter containing your full contact information.

Thanks for considering LDP and Ca$h Presents.

J-Blunt

PROLOGUE

Chino wasn't the biggest nigga in the world. Standing 6'2" and 170 pounds, he wasn't exactly little either - just skinny. He had dark skin, shoulder-length dreads, and eyes that never stopped searching his surroundings. Right now he was surrounded by his R.O.B. niggas, a.k.a., Ride Out Boyz. They were four deep in a Range Rover, rolling through the city, catching off their phones.

"Stop actin' like you only be fuckin' bad bitches, jackin'-ass nigga." Chino laughed. They were clowning R.O.B. Carti. The young pretty boy swore he only bagged dimes.

"On my soul, I don't fuck nothing basic, my nigga. I like my bitches foreign, like my whips. That be you niggas fuckin' these weave and wig wearin'-ass hoes."

"Nigga, you just fucked my bitch Tasha's sister a couple weeks ago," R.O.B. Spyder spoke up. "That bitch more basic than adding and subtracting."

Carti's face told it all. He had been caught in a lie. "What had happened was I was gone off them Percs. She light-skinned and it was dark in the club."

"I knew yo' hoe ass was lyin'. Soft-ass nigga." Chino laughed.

"My hoes still badder than yo' bitches, weak-ass nigga. Pull out yo' phone," Carti challenged.

"What? You ain't said nothing, nigga." Chino accepted, pulling out his phone. They were going through pictures of their females when Carti got a call.

"Matter of fact, this one of my bad ones right here. What up, baby?" he answered. After listening for a moment, he responded, "I'm out wit' my niggas. I ain't even driving right now." He listened for another moment. "A'ight. A'ight. I'm on my way," he said before hanging up. "Aye, Nitty. Ride over to that laundromat on Hopkins. I need to drop off some money to this bitch."

"Trickin'-ass nigga. That's the only way you can keep a bitch." Chino laughed.

"I might fuck a bitch and pay a bill!" Carti sang, pulling out a bankroll as thick as the Bible. "Come in and look at Michelle. Puerto Rican and Mexican. No weaves, nigga."

When Nitty pulled the van up to the laundromat, Carti dashed inside to take care of his girl. He came out a few moments later, eyes wide with surprise.

"Chino, you ain't gon' believe who in there right now."

"Who?"

Carti smiled, barely able to contain his enthusiasm. "That nigga that popped you. He in there right now."

Chino's face grew serious. "Crush in there right now? On what?"

"On everything I love. He fixing one of them dryers."

Chino pulled the .9 milli from his waist. After checking the chamber to make sure a bullet was ready, he got out of the Range. "I'm 'bout to get that bitch!"

"Hold on!" Spyder spoke up, looking around. "It's broad daylight and it's prolly cameras all around."

Chino ignored the warning, tucking the pistol into his waistband. "I don't give a fuck if Jesus was out here. I'm 'bout to get this bitch-ass nigga!"

"Get that fuck nigga!" Nitty cheered.

Chino walked towards the laundromat on a mission. He stopped at the big windows, trying to find Crush. First his eyes landed on the female he figured was Carti's bitch. Shorty was bad. Long hair, banging body, and she was fine. He saluted his li'l nigga in the back of his head, but didn't focus on the thought for too long. Then he spotted the target. Crush was wiping the sweat from his brow while standing over a dryer, a wrench in hand.

The old man could feel someone watching him. He looked up just in time to see Chino pull the heat and grab at the door. The old school gunslinger knew what time it was. Crush was trained to go. He went for the revolver tucked in the front of his pants as the bell above the front door began jingling. Unfortunately, he was too slow. Chino had the pistol pointed high, the barrel blazing fire.

Pop, pop, pop, pop, pop, pop, pop, pop!

Crush could feel the metal slugs hitting his body, tearing muscles and cracking bones. But that didn't stop him from pulling his shit and shooting back.

Boom, boom, boom, boom, boom!

Screams erupted from the laundromat patrons. Explosions from the .357 made Chino duck. Not wanting to be hit with one of the hollow points, the young gunner got out of there.

"Somebody call 9-1-1!" Crush screamed before falling to the floor.

J-Blunt

CHAPTER 1

The scene outside the laundromat tugged at Dro's heart. He didn't want to take another L to the streets. Police cars blocked off the parking lot and the laundromat was covered with yellow crime scene tape. People stood around talking to the police and recording with their cell phones. Dro brought the Charger to a screeching stop a few feet from the yellow tape. He hopped out and ran towards the front door. Police officers rushed towards him with their hands out, ready to take him down.

"Sir, get back!"

"Move! Get yo' hands off me! This my laundromat. Where my uncle?"

More police came to get in the skirmish and they tackled Dro to the ground.

"Sir, quit resisting! Calm down!"

"Let go of my muthafuckin' arm then! I just told y'all this my shit! Let me go!"

"Hey, what's going on out here?" an authoritative voice yelled, cutting through the ruckus.

"He was trying to come into the crime scene," an officer explained, bending Dro's arm.

"This my laundromat. I'm looking for Detective Hopkins."

"Let him go, guys. Let him up!" the man ordered.

They took their time letting him up, the desire for violence in the officer's eyes.

"You got a death wish, son?"

Dro looked to the man before him. Detective Darrell Hopkins was forty-seven years old, brown-skinned with a thick mustache, average height.

"Nah, them muthafuckas trippin'. Where my uncle?"

"Relax, man. I'm Detective Hopkins. Is Chris Patrick your uncle?"

"Yeah. Where he at?"

"At the hospital. He was shot multiple times. I need access to the video footage in the laundromat. Do you know who would want to hurt your uncle?"

Dro spun on his heels, heading for the Charger. "Nah, he don't got no enemies. I gotta get to the hospital."

"Hey, wait! Officer, don't let him leave!" Hopkins called.

Dro was rushed by two of the police he'd been in the scuffle with. "Stop! Don't get in that car!"

"What the fuck, man? Fuck y'all want?" Dro exploded, ready to take them all on.

The detective's face was serious and he was beginning to lose his cool. "I need that footage for the investigation. Your cooperation will make this go a lot smoother."

Realizing he was pissing everybody off and that he probably wouldn't leave until he gave them the footage, Dro cooperated. After giving Hopkins the video footage, he jumped in the Charger and sped from the lot. On the way to the hospital, he called Candice.

"Hey, Ruben."

"Uncle Crush got shot at the laundromat. He at the hospital."

Hurt and confusion sounded in her voice. "Oh, no! Oh, God, no! When did it happen? Is he okay?"

"I don't know. I'm on my way to the hospital right now. I just left the laundromat. The detective said he got shot more than once."

"Oh, God, no!" she cried. "Okay. I'm on my way. Oh, God!"

Hearing his aunty cry out to God made Dro call up to the heavens to say a prayer for the old man's life to be spared. Crush was a good nigga. He had quit the drugs and gotten his family back. To die before he got more time with them seemed wrong.

The vibration on his lap made him look at the phone. Forever's pretty face popped onto the screen.

"I'm not gon' make that flight, baby. My uncle got shot. I'm on my way to the hospital now."

She looked devastated. "No, Ruben, no! What happened?"

"I don't know. He got shot at the laundromat. The police called me."

"Why does this keep happening to us?"

12

Dro blew out a heavy breath. "I don't know, baby. But I'm tired of this shit. Every time I turn around, it's something else. Every time I try to leave, something happens that pulls me back."

"No, baby. You don't have to go back. You don't have to get involved. You can come to the airport. Or I can come get you. The plane doesn't leave for another hour. We have time. I'm coming to you."

"Nah, Forever. Get on the plane. Don't come to me. Go to North Dakota. Get away from this shit. If something happens to you or the baby, I wouldn't know what to do."

Forever was on the verge of tears. "But what about you? I want to be here for you. I want to be with you so you won't be alone."

"I'm okay, baby. Just knowing you and the baby safe is what I need right now. Get on that plane."

"Ruben, I don't want to leave without you. I'll wait for you. If you don't make it, I won't get on. I'll buy us some more tickets. I need you to come with me. I want you to be safe, too."

"I'm pulling up to the hospital now. Get on the airplane, Forever. I'ma call you when I finish checking on Crush."

The tears began spilling. "Ruben, please. I don't want to leave without you."

"Just go. I'ma be there."

"You promise? Are you gonna go for revenge again? I don't want you to. Let God fight the battle. I don't want you to get hurt or get in trouble."

"I'ma be fine. I love you."

"Wait. Ruben, promise me you won't get caught up in the revenge thing again. We need you."

He stared at her pretty face on the phone screen, knowing he couldn't make that promise. Whoever shot his uncle wasn't going to have to worry about hospitals, doctors, and surgery. He was sending them straight into the dirt.

"Get on the plane, baby. I'ma call you later."

***

Dro sat in the waiting room, mind running a million miles an hour. Crush was still in surgery, had been for two hours. The length of time the doctors were operating along with his uncle being forty-seven years old made Dro wonder if the old man's body could survive the trauma. Multiple gunshots didn't sound good. If Crush died, it would make the hole in his heart from Asia's loss bigger. God help the whole world if he lost another family member to the streets.

"Mom, is Daddy okay?"

Dro looked up as Kathy came rushing into the waiting room, tears spilling down her pretty face.

"He's in surgery, baby," Candice cried, locking her daughter into an embrace.

After the hug, Kathy turned to Dro for answers. "What happened? Who did it?"

"I don't know. I gave the police the video from the laundromat. They haven't said anything to me."

Candice sighed, wiping away tears from her eyes. "I can't believe two men that I knew got shot and killed so close to one another. It just doesn't seem real."

A white man in his early fifties walked into the waiting room. He wore a white coat and was flanked by a nurse. His face was grim with no signs of the news he was about to offer up. Dro stood to meet him.

"How he doing?"

"We did everything we could. Chris fought. He lost a lot of blood and died on the operating table a couple of times. But we kept bringing him back. Somehow he survived."

The family cheered, sharing a hug.

"He's out of it right now. He was shot six times all over the torso, multiple organs hit. Lungs, stomach, appendix. His intestines were shredded, but somehow he pulled through. I think it's a miracle that he survived. The Man upstairs wasn't ready to bring him home."

"Can we see him?" Candice asked, wiping away tears of happiness.

14

"In a moment. He's being transferred to a room in the ICU. He won't wake up for another hour or so and he'll be very weak. The surgery was delicate and he will need to rest. This is Nurse Mary. When he is settled in, she will be able to take you to the room."

"Thank you so much for saving my daddy," Kathy said, reaching out and hugging the doctor.

"You're welcome. But it wasn't me. You have to thank the Man in the sky for this one."

Ten minutes later, they were taken to Crush's room. The old man was lying on his back, sleeping. Tubes were in his nose, another hooked up to an IV in his arm. The sight pissed Dro off. Crush was his closest family. Just yesterday Crush was on his feet, viral, and strong. Now he was lying in a drug-induced fog, fighting for his life. The family members had seats and sat in silence, thankful for Crush to still be alive.

"What was my daddy doing when he was in the streets?" Kathy asked.

"I don't know," Dro lied.

"He said you took care of him while he was out there, but he wouldn't say what he did. You know what he was doing out there. Why don't you want to tell me?"

"Kathy, if yo' pops didn't tell you, you can't expect me to."

"He put that life behind him. That's all that matters," Candice added.

"That's not all that matters, Mom. Whatever Dad was doing is what probably got him shot. Somebody shot him six times, so this wasn't an accident. They tried to kill him. I want to know what he was into, and Ruben knows. So what is it, cousin?"

"If Crush didn't tell you, I won't either. That's his business, and you gotta take it up with him when he wakes up," Dro said.

"It's like that, for real?" Kathy asked, anger blazing in her eyes. "My sister got killed because of you, and now my dad gets shot at your laundromat. Everybody that messes with you gets shot. It's you that's the problem!"

"Kathy, stop!" Candice yelled. "Your father is hurt. You're not about to start this mess in his room. I know you're mad. I am too.

But taking it out on Ruben won't solve anything. Your father needs to rest."

"But don't you see, Momma? Ruben is the reason. He's the reason Savannah died. Ask him if he knows who killed her. All this time the police been tryna find a connection to the shooting and it's been him. Ask him."

Candice spun slowly towards her nephew, disbelief etched on her face. "What is she talking about? Is she right?"

Dro looked away, unable to take the blame showing in his aunt's eyes.

"Why didn't you tell the police so they could catch him? Why didn't you tell your family so we could have some answers and not believe some fool just started shooting?"

Dro let out a hot breath. He was mad that Kathy figured out everything and put him on the spot. "Because I took care of it. That's why."

"What does that even mean?" Kathy asked.

"Yeah, what does that mean?" Candice added.

"It means I killed that nigga!" Dro exploded, surprising them with the burst of anger. "I killed that nigga and his whole family. That's why I didn't tell the police. It's over with, and I don't wanna talk about this shit no more. Y'all ain't the only one that lost. My daughter got killed."

"What's going on?" Crush whispered weakly.

The family forgot about the argument and rushed to the bedside. "Daddy!"

"Hey, baby!"

"Unc, you good?"

"I'm okay. Take more than a couple bullets to get rid of me." He groaned. "What's all the noise about?"

Dro looked at Kathy and shook his head. "Everything good, Unc. We was just worried about you."

"Yeah, baby. We was worried about you," Candice said, kissing his cheek. "How are you feeling? Do you need me to call a nurse?"

"No. I'm good. I just needed to see y'all faces. I'ma be fine," he whispered.

"I was so scared, Daddy. Do you know who did it?"

The question got Dro's attention. Crush looked up and spoke with his eyes. Dro heard him.

"Nah, I don't know who did it. But the security cameras were recording."

"I gave it to the detectives," Dro said.

"Good," Crush breathed. "Hopefully they catch him soon."

After the women spent some time loving on their wounded protector, they left to use the bathroom and grab something to eat. As soon as the door closed, Dro asked the question he'd been dying to know the answer to since he got the call from Detective Hopkins.

"Was it Dirty?"

"Nah. It was Chino's bitch ass."

Dro frowned. "Who the fuck is Chino?"

"That nigga we robbed. It was my vic. I shot him in the stomach for humiliating me when I was out there bad."

Recognition flashed in Dro's eyes. "The black-ass nigga I gave the dope back to?"

"Yeah. Him. North side niggas. He with a clique called Ride Out Boyz."

"Don't trip, Unc. I'ma ride out on his bitch ass. I got it. Get well, nigga. I'ma come back to visit soon."

After leaving the hospital, Dro hopped in the car, trying to decide his next move. For the first time in a long time, he was on his own. Lunatic had moved to Atlanta. Twenty was locked up. Tae was dead. And Crush was in the hospital. If Chino was part of a clique, that meant he probably wouldn't be alone, which was fucked up because Dro didn't have any allies he trusted enough to take to war with him. But he couldn't let Crush's hit go unanswered. Chino had to get burned, as soon as possible. The only person he had counted on as of late was Shamika, and that's when he realized she was all he needed.

"What up, nigga? You remembered how good my pussy was and decided to stay?" Shamika answered the phone.

"Not exactly. Where you at?"

J-Blunt

"I'm at home. Isis 'bout to come pick me up. Why? You supposed to be on that plane, ain't you?"

"I'm not leaving. I got some unfinished business that I'm hoping you can help me with."

She sounded happy. "You know I got you, baby. Tell me what you need me to do."

***

"Damn! That bitch thick as fuck!" Nitty pointed.

The Ride Out Boyz looked in the direction of his finger. A short, light-skinned woman with blonde brushed waves was walking past their trap. She wore a powder blue short-sleeved midriff hoodie that showed off a flat stomach. Little cotton shorts fit her ass like spandex, showing off a ginormous booty that clapped every time she took a step.

"That bitch bad!" Chino whistled, jumping off the porch. "Aye, shorty! Hold on. Lemme holla at you."

"That bitch need to fuck wit' a nigga like me." Carti followed.

Shamika looked behind her and saw the niggas following like sharks that tasted blood in the water. "Uh-uh. What y'all niggas on?"

"Tryna see what up wit' you. Slow down," Carti said as he and Chino closed the distance.

Shamika didn't stop, continuing to play hard to get. "I got somewhere to be. What y'all want?"

"I wanna know why you walking?" Chino asked when he caught up to her. "You too bad to be out here by yo'self. You wanna ride?"

CHAPTER 2

"What it do, my nigga?" Dro answered the phone.

"On what, you did that shit to Tae?" Twenty asked, pain in his voice.

Dro lay his head against the head rest and closed his eyes. He knew this moment was coming, had known since he told Lunatic. But now that the moment was upon him, he wasn't ready.

"Man, Twenty. I couldn't let that shit go. He came to my house. Killed my dog. Tried to do me in."

"But you lied to us, my nigga. Looked us in the face and said it wasn't you. All along it was. What the fuck, Dro?"

"I don't know what you want me to say. What you woulda did if you was me? You sayin' you wouldn't fuck a nigga over that tried to get you out the way?"

Twenty was silent for a moment. "I wouldn't say all that. But that was our nigga. Our brother. All the shit we been through. I'm salty about this shit, my nigga. I wish you wouldn't have said shit and let us believe it was Dirty. Fucked up it had to be you. Why the fuck you didn't keep that shit to yo'self?"

"I don't know. I was drinking and we was keepin' it a hunnit. I regret how all that shit went down and I was tellin' Luna about it."

"Didn't you watch Dave Chappelle? This the kinda shit that happens when keepin' it real goes wrong. You can't keep it real all the time. Damn, Dro. We done already said too much on this phone and all this shit recorded. I just wanted you to know I'm salty about this shit. And I'm glad I'm locked up 'cause I don't know how shit would be if I found out when I was out."

Dro didn't like the threat behind his words. "Fuck that s'posed to mean, nigga?"

Twenty didn't bite his tongue. "Exactly what I said. That whole situation foul, brah. If I was out, with the way I'm feeling right now, we would've had to throw some hands over this. And I'm not sayin' this just because it's you. If Tae woulda got down on you, I would be sayin' the same shit. I don't got no blood brothers, so you niggas is my family. Shit, and losing my nigga hurt. I don't give a fuck if you don't like what I'm sayin'. You hurt yo' niggas. If my words hurt you, shit, now you know how we feel."

Dro thought about Twenty's words and realized he wasn't talking shit, but keeping it real. He wasn't trying to be disrespectful, but expressing his anger about the situation.

"I hear you, brah. I do. I just couldn't let that shit go."

"I already know. But we gon' figure it out. You still my nigga. On some other shit, did you move to North Dakota yet?"

Dro let out a breath. "Nah, brah. Crush got popped up and I'm tryna find the nigga that did it."

"On what, Crush got hit up? You know who did it?"

"Yeah. I'm on that."

"Damn, my nigga. I wish I was out there with you, brah. Be careful. Brandon working on tryna get these charges dropped. When I get out this bitch, it's on. I'ma Don Kaluminati seven day theory all my enemies."

"Damn, my nigga. Didn't you just talk about this shit being recorded?"

"Hell yeah. But sometimes I just don't give no fuck. I know Forever pissed you didn't come with her. Y'all bout to have a baby and shit. Do you know what y'all havin; yet?"

"Nah. Won't find out 'til her next appointment. And yeah, she mad. But I gotta get to the bottom of this shit."

"I hear you, my nigga. But like I said, be careful."

"I am. You know Savages stay dangerous."

***

"These niggas look grimy. You sure they got some money?" Isis asked. She was a friend of Shamika's. They danced together at Silk's and sometimes got money together on the side. Although she didn't have the big booty or big breasts that all strippers wanted nowadays, Isis was a hustler and had crazy sex appeal. She looked more like a high fashion model than an exotic dancer. Plus, she was fine: unblemished dark skin, chinky eyes, high cheekbones, and green dreadlocks that hung to the middle of her back. Standing six

20

feet tall, with a slim build and small breasts, she knew how to use what she had to get what she wanted.

"We good, baby. These the Ride Out Boyz. They got a li'l money. Plus I already got the band for us just showing up. Relax. Let's go out here and get these niggas' money. Quit trippin'."

"A'ight. If you say so. How you wanna play this one?"

Shamika smiled. "Just grab that bag and follow my lead. We about to put on a show that these niggas will die for."

The women left the room wearing bathrobes with panties and bras underneath. The Ride Out Boyz sat around the living room, eager to see the sexy show that Shamika promised.

"'Bout time y'all came out here. I was 'bout to come in that bitch." Nitty said, eyeing the women lustfully.

"Well, I hope you niggas got another pair of draws 'cause y'all about to nut in them when y'all see me and my bitch get down," Shamika promised.

"Quit talkin' and let me see what you talkin' 'bout," Chino spoke up.

Shamika untied the front of the robe, striking a pose. "Ask and you shall receive, baby."

Both women let the robes fall to the floor and did a sexy walk around the room so the men could get a look at their goodies. Carti slapped Shamika on the ass when she walked by. The clique oooh'd and ahhh'd at how her big light-skinned booty shook. Then the women met in the middle of the room, pawing at one another's body while sharing a sexy kiss. After laying the robes down like a pallet, Shamika grabbed the bag Isis set on the floor.

"Get naked and lay down."

Isis lay down on the robes while Shamika opened the bag of goodies. Inside were sex toys, oils, and candles. After lighting the candle, she pulled out a bottle of oil and squirted some in her hands before rubbing it on Isis's body, paying a lot of attention to her little heart-shaped booty. When her body was good and oiled up, she rolled Isis onto her back and covered her eyes with a blindfold. Shamika grabbed the oil again, standing over Isis and squirting it all over. When she was covered in oil, Shamika bent down and rubbed it into her skin. Then she straddled her and began sucking her small titties.

"Mmm!" Isis moaned.

The Ride Out Boyz were mesmerized by the sex show playing out on the floor before them. None of them blinking, all of them rocking tents in the crotch of their jeans. Shamika continued to work her mouth all over Isis's body. Then she grabbed the candle and began pouring a trail of hot wax from her stomach up to her neck.

"Ahhhh! Ssss!" Isis moaned, caught between pleasure and pain. Shamika rubbed the hot wax over Isis's body before kneeling between and spreading her legs wide. The Ride Out Boyz watched Shamika play with the pretty pinkness. Then she dove in, licking her girl's pussy like an expert. She sucked her pearl tongue while fingering her. When Isis was good and wet, she stuck out her tongue and pushed it in her ass, fucking her with it like her tongue was a small dildo.

Isis went crazy. "Oh, shit! Ahh! Ahhhh!"

Next Shamika went back into the bag and pulled out an eight inch strap-on dildo. After putting it on, she pushed Isis's legs to her chest again and climbed on top. She slipped deep inside, pausing to look at Isis's sex face.

"Ssss! Oh, shit!" Isis moaned.

"Y'all wanna watch me fuck the shit out of her?" she asked the group of horny men.

"Hell yeah!" they cheered.

"You want this dick?" Shamika asked Isis.

"Yeah, baby. Fuck me good, bitch. Beat this pussy up."

Shamika held Isis's legs to her chest and fucked her like the dick was real. She hit it fast, then changed to slow, long strokes before picking up speed again.

"Ahh, shit! Damn, bitch. Don't stop. Don't stop. I'm finna cum!" Isis called.

Shamika kept up the fast stroke until Isis began screaming, body shivering. But the show wasn't over. She flipped Isis onto her knees and held the fake dick near her ass. When she looked up at the Ride Out Boyz, they all looked ready to bust a nut.

22

"Y'all want me to fuck her in the ass?"

"Hell yeah!" they cheered again.

Shamika spread Isis's cheeks wide, spitting on her asshole before working the dildo in.

"Ssss, Mmmhhh! Yeah, bitch. Damn," Isis moaned.

Shamika started off slow, giving her the dick inch by inch until she was deep inside her anal walls. It wasn't long before she was tearing that ass up. She grabbed ahold of Isis's dreads and slapped her ass, dicking her girl down.

"Oh, gawd! Oh gawd! Damn, bitch!" Isis moaned, grabbing handfuls of the robe.

After Isis came again, Shamika pulled out and stood over her with the shit-stained dildo.

"Open yo' mouth. Clean me off."

Isis opened her mouth, sticking out her tongue as Shamika pushed the dildo all the way down her throat. She fucked her tonsils until the dildo was clean.

"How y'all like that?" Shamika asked the crowd.

"That shit was fiya!" Chino cheered.

"Y'all shoulda let niggas record that," Nitty said, grabbing hold of his dick through his pants.

"I wanna know if I can fuck?" Carti asked, eyeing Shamika.

"Sorry, my nigga. This was a business thang. But if you wanna get up later, we can."

"A'ight. Hold on. What is it gon' take to watch you get fucked, Shamika?" Chino asked.

Shamika looked down at Isis. "Can you handle all this ass?"

"I'll fuck you betta than you ever been fucked in yo' life."

Shamika looked to Chino. "I need another band for y'all to watch her pop my pussy."

After another sex show on the living room floor, the women retired to the bathroom to clean up. During the intermission, Shamika sent a text to Dro.

"Baby, hurry up and put yo; clothes on. We gon' have to climb out this bathroom window."

Isis looked at her like she was crazy. "Bitch, you trippin'. I ain't about to climb out no window."

Shamika got serious. "Trust me on this, baby. We gotta go. Some shit finna pop off in a couple minutes and we can't be here when it happens."

The sound of her friend's voice made Isis nervous. "Girl, what did you get me into?"

"Nothing. Just put on yo' shit and let's climb out this window."

****

Dro read the text from Shamika and smiled. Three Ride Out Boyz were in the house. The odds were stacked heavily against him, but he didn't even think of turning back. Three against one sounded like he might take an L. But he had something they didn't: the element of surprise. Concealed by the night and wearing no mask, he crept through the alley, holding the AK-47 with the hundred round drum at the ready. When he got to the house, the women were climbing out of the bathroom window. Isis was startled when she saw him with the chopper.

"Dro, what the fuck you doing?"

"Shut up. Get to the car and wait for me," he told her before turning to Shamika. "Where them niggas at?"

Excitement shone in her eyes. "They in the living room waiting for us to come out the bathroom."

"Make sure the car running," he told her before climbing into the bathroom window. He took a moment to gather himself before going on the mission. The bathroom was near the back of the house, in a short hallway.

As soon as he opened the door, he turned left and seen his first victim. Carti tried to scream.

"Oh shi-"

Tat-tat-tat-tat-tat-tat-tat!

Carti didn't even get to finish the warning. The high-powered rifle bullets slammed into his chest, cutting the young man down where he stood. Dro didn't wait for the body to hit the ground before he was on the move again. He raced towards the living room. Chino jumped up from the couch and drew heat. They saw each other at the same time.

Clap, clap, clap, clap!

Tat-tat-tat-tat-tat-tat!

The bullets barely missed Dro, forcing him to take cover. Chino wasn't so lucky. Chopper bullets hit him in the chest and shoulder, knocking him to the floor.

"Ah, shit!" the Ride Out Boy moaned, crawling behind the couch, out of Dro's line of sight.

Dro smiled at the cry of the wounded. Excitement from the thrill of the kill pushed him on. He jumped around the corner, ready to kill, and saw another man coming from the bedroom holding a Mini-14. Ride Out Boy Nitty began spraying 223 bullets as Dro let the AK-47 ride.

Tat-tat-tat-tat-tat-tat!

Brrrrreaaaaatttt!

Both men missed before ducking around corners, out of sight. Not wanting to leave without bodying Chino, Dro stuck his head around the corner, trying to get a bead on one of the Ride Out Boyz. Nitty peeked out just enough to see Dro peeking at him. Both men lifted their guns again and began spraying.

Tat-tat-tat-tat-tat-tat!

Brrrrreaaaaatttt! Brrrrreaaaaatttt!

Realizing he wasn't going to get his man, Dro did the only thing he could and ran to the bathroom. After leaping out the window, he ran for the car parked a block away. Isis was in the driver's seat, Shamika the passenger.

"Go, go, go!" he yelled, jumping in the backseat.

"Did you get them niggas? How much we get? I'm ready to get paid." Shamika grinned, her eyes flashing excitement.

"Don't even lean on that. Y'all did y'all part. Leave it alone. I'ma pay y'all when we get to the house."

"What the fuck y'all got me out here doing? I don't wanna be part of no robbery shit. Why didn't y'all tell me what the fuck was going on?" Isis panicked as she sped away.

Dro gave Shamika a look, ready to kill both of them if necessary. "What's up with yo' girl?"

"She good. Chill, Isis. He just robbed them niggas. It ain't like he killed nobody."

CHAPTER 3

Dirty sat in the passenger seat of the Benz truck smoking a blunt. His eyes darted back and forth, watching for anything out of the ordinary as the SUV rode through the Milwaukee streets. He was beginning to love the city. The griminess reminding him of home. Since he'd been in the Brew City, the body count around him piled up. He was saddened by the loss of Cherry and his cousin, Eddie, but comforted by the money their deaths put in his pocket. And now that he was part of Coupe's team, it didn't seem like money would be a problem anymore.

"I think you should fuck up Bam-Bam. I don't like that li'l bitch-ass nigga," Coupe said.

Dirty eyed his benefactor. Coupe was a little nigga, barely above five feet tall and skinny. He had brown skin, an uncombed afro, and gold teeth.

"Why you got him on yo' team if you don't like him?"

"Levi did that shit."

"The li'l nigga is good. You just mad 'cause he taller than you," the lesbian cracked from the back seat.

Levi looked like she could be Coupe's twin. Both were short, skinny, and had gold teeth. The only things that separated them was Levi's brushed waves and that Coupe had a set of balls and a dick.

"And he soft as a bitch," Coupe said. "Nigga got robbed and they had pistols in the house. I ain't going for that shit. Nigga prolly spent the money and lying and saying he got robbed. Fuck the nigga up, Dirty."

"Nah, Dirty. Don't touch my li'l nigga," Levi said.

"I'ma let y'all figure out what to do wit the li'l nigga. I ain't with disciplining niggas. I just wanna know who robbed him so I can get down on some niggas."

When the Benz trucked pulled to the curb outside the bando, the trio climbed from the luxurious SUV. Dirty towered over his counterparts like David did Goliath. The prison workouts had the goon built like he played professional sports and he moved with the swagger of a certified gangsta. They walked in the house and Coupe got right on the two hustlers' asses.

"What the fuck happened?"

"Caught us slippin' and ran in," Bam-Bam answered.

"What the fuck that mean? Why the fuck was you niggas slippin'? You know to be ready at all times. What the fuck I be telling y'all?"

Bam-Bam hung his head. Travis didn't even speak up for himself. Neither of the young men had been raised in the streets like most drug dealers. Bam-Bam was about to turn twenty-one and grew up in a working class community. Once he got a taste of the street life, he wanted more. Travis was nineteen. He had hoop dreams, but a gang rape charge took him out of the game. Now he was hustling to make a way. Neither man had answers for Coupe, and the sight of their softness and lack of aggression incensed him.

"You niggas don't hear me? Tell me exactly what the fuck happened. How much they take?" he snapped, grabbing Bam-Bam by the collar.

Bam-Bam was a few inches taller than Coupe and outweighed him by at least twenty-five pounds, but the younger man didn't even think about challenging his boss.

"Two hundred fifty grams and sixty racks."

"How the fuck they get in the house? And why you niggas ain't pop they ass, or at least shoot?"

"I thought it was some action. When I opened the door, three niggas had pistols in my face. Travis was on the couch asleep."

Coupe looked to Levi. She shrugged her shoulders, unsure how to handle the situation.

"Did y'all know the niggas?" Dirty spoke up.

"Nah, we don't know 'em but I seen the car they got away in. I think it's them niggas from over on Bender," Travis answered.

Coupe mugged both youngsters. "Let me find out y'all set me up and I'm smokin' y'all li'l bitch asses. What the niggas look like?"

"I don't know. They wore masks. But they was tall and had dreads. Had dark skin," Bam-Bam said.

28

Coupe looked suspicious. "They wore a mask, but you seen all that, huh?"

"I seen they arms. They was tatted."

"What kinda car was it?" Dirty asked.

"A green Chevy on chrome."

"Where them pistols we gave y'all?" Levi asked.

Travis pointed to the couch. "They was under there."

"So, you mean to tell me that y'all had heat and didn't buss?" Coupe asked, looking like he wanted to hurt the youngsters.

Bam-Bam tried to rationalize their actions. "We couldn't get to 'em. And I didn't wanna run outside shooting because they was already driving off and it might've made the neighbors call the police."

"I don't give a fuck about them bitch-ass neighbors! When a nigga violate you, you fuck 'em up! No matter if yo' mama standing right there or the mu'fuckin' president. You don't let niggas get at you and not do nothing about it. That's some bitch shit!" Coupe yelled, reaching back and slapping Bam-Bam.

That got the youngster fired up. "Don't be puttin' yo' hands on me, nigga!" he yelled, grabbing Coupe and pushing him into the wall.

For a split second, fear shone in Coupe's eyes. The youngster was bigger and stronger. And Coupe wasn't a fighter.

Dirty grabbed the big young'un, separating him from the boss. "A'ight, li'l nigga. Don't put yo' hands on my boy."

"Fuck that nigga up! Pop his bitch ass!" Coupe yelled at Dirty.

"Don't, Dirty." Levi shook her head before turning to Bam-Bam. "You can't be puttin yo' hands on the boss, li'l nigga."

Bam-Bam huffed and puffed, mugging Coupe. "Tell that nigga not to be puttin' his hands on me then. We got robbed. We told y'all who did it. We didn't do nothin' wrong."

"Yes, you did. You being a bitch is what's wrong," Coupe snapped. "You let them niggas take my shit and I want it back. Every dolla. And every gram. Get my shit, li'l nigga!"

***

After leaving the trap, Coupe, Levi, and Dirty hopped in the Benz to ride around and check another house.

"How you expect that nigga to pay you the money and dope without no product?" Levi asked.

"I was wondering the same thing." Dirty chuckled.

"That ain't my problem. Li'l bitch ass nigga betta come up with my shit is all I know," Coupe huffed.

"Why don't you just give the nigga some shit and have him work it for free? He our worker and can't work if he don't got no work," Levi said.

"Bitch-ass nigga ain't working for us no more. And that nigga betta have my shit or I need you to fuck him up, Dirty."

"Whatever, man," Dirty said, blowing him off. "I'm more worried about these Bender niggas. They the ones that violated. You and Levi discipline yo' own workers."

A phone call made Levi step back from the convo. "What up, Angie?" After listening for a moment, she got mad. "Where that nigga at right now? Okay, I'm on my way."

"What was that about?" Coupe asked when he heard the rise in her tone.

"Zero on some bullshit again. Go by the nigga's house so I can stop this fool-ass nigga from going to jail or gettin' killed."

"You can't keep on savin; this nigga," Dirty spoke up. "I know that's yo' brotha, but he starting to become more of a burden than anything."

Levi took a moment to ponder the words. The OG was right. "I'ma take care of it. Just take me over there, Coupe."

When the SUV pulled up to the house Zero shared with his girl, Angie, the scene spoke for itself. Neighbors stood around looking towards the porch of the gray and black house. Zero was a tall, dark=skinned nigga with a bushy beard. He wore no shirt over his thin tattooed chest as he kicked on the front door, seemingly throwing a tantrum.

"Zero!" Levi screamed as she climbed from the truck. "What the fuck you doing?"

The shirtless man spun around at the sound of her voice. "This punk-ass bitch playing games with me. I'll kill this bitch, sis!"

"Bro, you tripping," Levi said angrily as she walked upon the porch. "You got all these people out here watching you act a fool. C'mon, man. You tripping. They might be calling the police. Get in the truck."

He became defiant. "Fuck that shit! This bitch finna open this mu'fuckin' door and tell me why that nigga was all in her face."

"What nigga? What is you talkin' 'bout?"

"At the restaurant. Bitch showing a nigga all her teef, laughing and having a good time. I ain't stupid. Bitch ain't finna clown me."

"C'mon, bro. Just get in the car. We can talk about this with her later. Right now, I need to keep you out of jail. C'mon."

Agreeing with his sister's reasoning, Zero walked towards the Benz truck.

A black old school Monte Carlo on chrome wheels came fishtailing around the corner. It sped down the block and came to a screeching stop in the middle of the street. The driver and passenger hopped out, wearing aggressive looks. The passenger also had a bulge in the front of his shirt.

"You put yo' hands on my sister, nigga!?" A-Love mugged, walking towards Zero.

Dirty climbed from the truck, watching to see how everything would play out.

"Bitch-ass nigga, don't be comin' over here like you finna get down!" Zero snapped, throwing up his hands and walking towards the armed man.

A-Love took a wild swing at Zero, missing by a mile. Zero swung back, busting him in his shit. The driver of the Monte Carlo got in the fray and punched Zero, forcing Levi to defend her little brother. She punched the nigga in the mouth, drawing blood. Needing to protect his money bag holder, Dirty got in the mix and took a swing at the driver. The punch was fast and landed perfectly on the man's jaw. He fell to the ground like a robot that had its power cut off. Zero was in a wrestling match with A-Love, trying to stop him from reaching the pistol in his waist. Not wanting to be involved in a broad daylight body, Dirty snatched the nigga away from Zero and threw him into the Benz truck. He hit the SUV head first and fell to the ground. Before he could figure out what was happening and what to do about it, Dirty grabbed him by the shirt, lifting him from the ground. He ripped the pistol from A-Love's pants and pointed it to his head.

"Check this out, li'l nigga. You gon' pick yo' nigga up and get the fuck outta here before you piss me off and I blow yo' shit off! Fuck outta here, nigga!"

When Dirty released the young punk, he stumbled over to his boy. After a few slaps to the face, he woke up, still dazed.

"C'mon, brah. We gotta go," A-Love said as they scrambled to the Monte Carlo and sped away.

After tucking the pistol, Dirty turned to Zero. "Get'cho ass in the truck, soft-ass nigga. Got us out here on some fuck shit 'cause you in yo' feelin's over a bitch. Sensitive-ass nigga."

"Is Angie's pussy really that good?" Coupe laughed as he drove away from the domestic scene.

"Ain't no pussy in the world good enough to be dyin' or killin' for," Levi commented.

"It ain't even about the pussy," Zero defended himself. "It's about the principal. These niggas ain't showin' no respect and these hoes need to know how to act. Sometimes you gotta beat a bitch."

"You just need to stop being a pussy whipped-ass nigga," Dirty jumped in. "You don't let no pussy have you out there actin a fool, li'l nigga. Nigga, if you get locked up over this bitch, you think she gon' stop fucking niggas? Hell nah. She gon' be fuckin' more 'cause you ain't around to stop her. Let a hoe be a hoe."

"Preach, my nigga! Tell that shit!" Coupe laughed.

"C'mon, Coupe. That cheerleading shit ain't cool," Levi spoke up for her little brother.

"Well, tell that nigga to get off this sucka shit. Nigga need to put that energy towards gettin' a bag. I need niggas out here making sure our money good. Need niggas out here looking for them Savage niggas. That nigga Dro still out here runnin' round. Matter fact, this what you do, li'l brah. I got fifty bands on that nigga's head.

Focus yo' energy on that instead of chasin' a bitch. How you love that?"

The truck became silent for a moment. Zero couldn't help but think about fifty G's lining his pockets.

"Tell me more about this nigga, Dro. Where he be at?"

"Used to be over on Garfield, but ain't nobody seen him since Dirty got on them niggas' ass."

Zero turned to Dirty. "You know how to get at this nigga?"

"I did. But he in hiding now. He got a couple laundromats that I been checkin' out. And we know where his li'l bitch live. But I ain't seen him."

"Show me where the bitch live. I'ma lamp on that bitch. I need that fifty in my pocket."

Coupe smiled, liking the young'un's eagerness. "Say no more, li'l nigga. We bout to get over there right now. Dirty, this li'l nigga might be tryna take yo spot. Look out."

Coupe parked the truck a couple houses away from Shamika's and they sat to watch the scene. Had been waiting for about ten minutes when the black Charger pulled to the curb out front. Shamika climbed from the car, followed by Isis.

"Y'all see that?" Levi pointed.

"Yeah," Dirty spoke up. "The light-skinned one is his bitch. But I haven't been able to see him come over here."

"Why don't we just get the bitches and make them tell us where the nigga at? Shit, we can take care of this right now," Zero said.

Coupe turned to look at Dirty. "What you wanna do?"

Dirty let out a breath. "A'ight. Give them hoes a little time to settle in."

J-Blunt

CHAPTER 4

Dro sat on the sofa, contemplating his next move. The shit with the Ride Out Boyz didn't go as planned. Chino survived. That was fucked up because it only added to his list of enemies. And as far as allies, he didn't have any. All his niggas were in fucked-up situations. He was against all odds. Enemies on every side. He thought about how he got to this point. Twice he made plans to leave the streets, and both times he was pulled back in. If it wasn't one thing, it was another. Made him wonder whether or not he would make it out alive. The story of Job came to mind. Forever had mentioned the biblical patriarch several times. They had a lot in common. Like Job, he got back everything he lost and then some. But unlike Job, he didn't get the happy ending. Drama was still chasing him and he didn't know how to explain this last set of events. He had a good woman that loved him, plus a baby on the way. He wanted to be with them, but the bullshit kept him riding solo. He needed to figure out a way to end this shit so he could be with his family. The one thing he didn't want to do was bring this shit to their doorstep. The best way to keep them safe was to stay away, and that was killing him. The buzz of his phone made him look down. Forever's pretty face shown on the screen.

"Hey, baby. I was just thinking about you."

"Me too. What are you doing? Are you still in bed?"

"Yeah. I don't got nothing going on today. Probably go see Crush later."

"How is he doing? Is he better?"

"He okay. Doc n'em said he gon' make a full recovery."

"That's good. I was worried about him and how you would react if he didn't make it."

"He good. I'm just laying here thinking."

"Penny for your thoughts."

"I wanna be home with you. I'm tryna figure out the best way to make that happen, but I don't know."

"Why can't you just get on a plane and leave?"

"Because I'm in it too deep. And I don't wanna put you and the baby in harm's way. I'm scared that if I leave shit the way it is, they might come looking for me. I don't wanna put you in danger again. I don't wanna lose nobody else to this street shit."

She sighed. "I hear you, baby. I just love you so much and want you here with me. But I don't want to put the baby at risk. Baby, what are we gonna do?"

"Just let me figure this out. I'm trying, baby. I swear I am."

Forever wiped the tears that spilled down her face. The sight of her sadness tugged at Dro's heartstrings.

"You have to make it back to us, Ruben. I don't want to raise our baby without you."

"I promise, I'm coming home. I just need a little more time. But I'm coming."

"This baby is making my emotions crazy. I go from laughing to crying in an instant. I'm worried about you and that is stressing me out. I always pictured the prefect family whenever I had a baby. Life is crazy."

"Don't stress, baby. You know that's bad for the baby. Believe me, Forever. I'm coming home."

"I believe you. Another thing this baby is doing is making my hormones crazy. And I'm horny all the time. I've never wanted sex so much. I thought something was wrong with me, but the doctor said it's normal."

Dro raised an eyebrow. "Where yo' daddy at?"

She squinted, mischief showing in her pretty brown eyes. "At work. Why?"

He removed the sheet, showing his nakedness. His dick was growing by the second. "Because seeing you makes me want to fuck you all the time."

"Ruben!" She blushed.

"I love when you say my name like that. Say it again, but sexy."

"Ruben, what has gotten into you?"

"You. Now say my name sexy."

She closed her eyes and moaned. "Oh, Ruben!"

Dro smiled. "That shit was sexy. Now show me yours."

36

She frowned. "Show you what?"

"Everything. Take yo' clothes off."

"Ruben, I don't think - "

"Stop thinking and do it. I wanna have phone sex with you. Take yo' clothes off. I miss you and I wanna see you. All of you."

Lust and excitement showed on her face. "Okay. Let me set the phone so you can see."

After positioning the phone, she stood and began taking off the sweat pants.

"Wait, baby," he stopped her. "Undress slow. Tease me. Be my stripper and dance for me like the Beyoncé song."

Forever didn't know anything about stripping, but she was going to try for her man. She moved seductively to a rhythm that played in her head, shimmying out of the sweats. Next came the T-shirt. Then she struck a few poses to show off her pregnant belly and engorged breasts. Dro grinned like a kid seeing porn for the first time as he watched his baby mama's strip tease.

"Turn around and bend over and slap that ass."

Forever spun around, showing her perfect light-skinned bubble butt. After bending over, she gave herself a spank. A wave rippled through her flesh. Dro's hand gripped his tool and began stroking.

"Lay down and let me see you play with that pussy."

She grabbed the phone and lay down. "Let me watch you first. I wanna see you masturbate."

Dro angled the phone so she could watch him get busy. "I'm picturing you riding me right now. Yo' pussy so good, baby. Damn, I love fucking you! Let me see you play with it."

Forever spread her legs and propped the phone so he could see everything. One hand spread her labia while the other went to work on her clit. She pleased herself while watching him stroke his dick.

"Oh, Ruben! I want you so bad, baby. Oh, my God!"

"Suck them titties for me, baby. Put 'em in yo' mouth. Imagine those my lips and tongue all over yo' body." He groaned.

Forever used her forearm to push the melons towards her mouth. Then she lifted her head and began licking her nipples. She moved her tongue back and forth, paying each nipple attention. Her moans got louder and her fingers moved faster across her clit as the orgasm built up. Dro was also experiencing similar pleasure. Watching Forever play with her pussy and suck her titties was erotic as fuck.

"Damn, baby. I'm 'bout to bust. You sexy as hell," he moaned.

"Oh, Ruben! Mmmm, baby! Let me see you cum. I wanna see."

"Oooh, shhhiiittt!" he groaned as white cream erupted from his piece, running down his fist and splashing onto his abs.

The sight was too much for Forever and she came hard. "Oh, God! Oh, Ruben, baby! Oh!"

"That shit was fire, baby!" Dro cheesed.

Forever wore a similar smile. "That was so erotic, baby. And that was the first time I ever had phone sex. Wow!"

"We might have to do this more often. Get you some toys."

"I don't know about all that." She laughed. "I'm a fan of the real thing, not toys."

"You don't know what you like until you try it. Probably never pictured yo'self having phone sex either. And now that you did it, you see it ain't that bad. Do it for yo' man."

She shook her head. "Oh, my God, Ruben. I don't know what I'm going to do with you."

"You gon' love me. Let me call you back. I gotta get this nut off me."

"Yeah, you nasty, but I like it. Love you, baby."

"I love you, too."

Dro went to the bathroom to take a quick shower. He was drying off when the front door opened. He poked his head out the bathroom door just in time to see Shamika walking in the house, followed by Isis.

"What you doing?" Shamika asked when she saw him peeking out the door.

"Seeing who was coming in the house."

"Oh, Dro. I need to get in there. I gotta use the bathroom so bad," Isis said, doing the I-gotta-pee dance.

After wrapping himself in a towel, he stepped into the hallway. On the way in the bathroom, Isis checked him out, her eyes pausing briefly at the bulge in the towel. They exchanged flirty looks before she closed the door.

"Damn, nigga. You ain't making it no secret, huh?" Shamika asked, watching the exchange.

He owned it. "Shit, you shoulda seen how she was looking at my dick. Like she could see through the towel."

Shamika looked down at his bulge and reached out to grab it. "Yo' shit do look good. Thanks for letting me use your car. Here go the keys."

When she tried to hand him the keys, he grabbed her hand, pulling her close. After wrapping her in a hug, he gripped her phatty. "Don't be grabbin' my shit if you ain't gon' do nothin' wit' it."

She copped a fake attitude, pushing him away. "Get'cho hands off me, nigga. Tell yo' new bitch, Isis, to take care of that."

"A'ight." He chuckled. "Don't tempt me."

Something like a challenge shown in her eyes. "I dare you to try to fuck her. I know what that pussy taste like. You don't."

Even though he had just finished busting a nut and wasn't't really that attracted to Isis, something about the challenge made him want to fuck Shamika's friend. When the bathroom door opened, he spun towards Isis, blocking her path. He looked her over, checking out her slim build in the flowing yellow sundress.

"You think you can handle me?"

She frowned, not understanding. "What you on, Dro?"

"You looked me up and down before you went in the bathroom. I wanna know if you think you can handle me."

She let out a nervous laugh, looking down at the bulge in the towel again. "C'mon, Dro. You fuck with my girl. What you doing, man?"

He closed the distance between them, pressing his crotch into her pelvis. She was six feet tall so they were almost eye to eye, their lips a few inches apart. "Yo' girl ain't trippin'. She standing right behind me. What up?"

Isis peeked her head out the bathroom and saw her friend watching. Shamika didn't look mad, but interested. After turning back to Dro, Isis smiled, cocking her head to the side. "Shit, what up, nigga?"

He grabbed her around the waist, forcing her into the bathroom as his lips found hers. The kiss was aggressive and highly sexual. After throwing her upon the sink, the towel fell to the floor. She grabbed his tool and began stroking him. He pulled the sundress over her head, discovering she didn't have on panties or a bra. His lips moved to suck her rock hard nipples.

"Oh, yeah!" she moaned, rubbing the back of his head.

Shamika walked to the doorway to watch. Dro couldn't see the look on her face, but Isis did. The women exchanged knowing smiles before Isis reached down and grabbed his dick again. She wanted it inside her walls. Dro obliged, lifting one of her legs on his shoulder and diving deep. She was hot and slippery wet. He wasn't worried about busting quickly since he had got one off with Forever. He punished the pussy, drilling her like a jackhammer on a construction site.

"Oh, shit! Damn, Dro! Yeah, nigga, get it!" Isis cheered, watching the horny look on Shamika's face.

The blonde-haired big booty queen was turned on, licking her lips as she watched the show.

Beads of sweat popped onto Dro's forehead as he deep stroked Isis. Her pussy was so good that he wanted to go deeper. After pushing the other leg onto his shoulder, he went ham. Isis held onto the sink, loving the way he was delivering the D.

"Mmmm, yeah! Oh, yeah! Oh, yeah!"

When his legs got tired from standing, he sat down on the toilet. Isis climbed on top, reverse cowgirl. Wanting to fuck him good, she contracted her pussy muscles, riding him fast and hard.

Deciding she'd done enough spectating, Shamika snatched off her stretch pants and got in on the action. She walked in front of Isis and lifted a leg onto the tub, pushing her pussy into her friend's face. Isis didn't miss a beat. She sucked Shamika's pussy and put it down on top of Dro. After Shamika came, she dropped to her knees and began sucking Isis's clit while she rode Dro.

"Oh, shit! Oh, shit! Ahhhh!" Isis screamed, sitting down and wetting Dro's lap as she came.

After another round of freaky-ass shower sex, the trio retired to the bedroom and continued to get their freak on. When they were done, the satisfied fuckers lay back and got high.

"Damn, that's the kinda fuckin' I wanna do." Isis smiled. "Fuck you been all this time, nigga?" she asked, rubbing Dro's abs.

"Waiting on you. Shit, I think we should do this all the time. What you say, Shamika?"

She took a puff on the blunt and blew out a big cloud of smoke. "You know I'm with it, baby. I love eating pussy and sucking dick. If I can do 'em both at the same time, I'm game."

"There it is, baby. You in." Dro grinned.

The ringing of the doorbell interrupted their good vibes.

"Damn. Who the fuck is this?" Shamika griped, getting out of bed and throwing on Dro's T-shirt.

"You expecting somebody?" he asked.

"Nah. It bet' not be no stupid shit or I'ma be pissed off."

The doorbell rang several more times, the person outside getting impatient.

"Hold the fuck on! Here I come!" Shamika yelled, storming angrily towards the door.

Something in Dro's gut didn't feel right. Everything that he'd been through over the last six months heightened his senses. Instead of second guessing, he trusted his instincts. He grabbed the Glock off the bedside table and made sure a bullet was in the chamber.

"Watch out, Isis."

She looked scared. "Why you grabbin' that?"

Before he could respond, Shamika screamed.

"Aaaahhhh!"

Dro bolted out of bed and raced towards the bedroom door, not caring that he was naked. When he got to the hallway, two niggas were forcing their way into the house. Both had pistols. One was tall and dark-skinned with a thick beard. The other nigga was tall, dark-skinned, and muscular. He had a bald head and a fluffy beard. Dro immediately recognized him from the club security camera footage that Whisper showed him. It was Dirty. They noticed Dro a split second too late. Surprise flashed in their eyes when the solo Savage lifted the pistol and started shooting.

Pop, pop, pop, pop, pop, pop, pop, pop!

The first nigga's reaction was too slow. He was shirtless and Dro could see the bullets punching into the flesh of his chest. Dirty was much quicker, moving on instinct. He backed out of the house, firing shots and forcing Dro to step out of his line of sight.

Clap, clap, clap, clap, clap!

"Aahhhhh!" Shamika screamed, falling to the floor.

Dro continued moving towards the door, keeping the pistol ready. When he looked outside, Dirty was gone. After locking the door, he spun to check the damage. Dirty's boy was shaking like he was having a seizure, blood leaking from the holes in his chest. Shamika lay on her stomach, moaning in agony.

"Where you hit at?" he asked, kneeling down and rolling her over.

The sight was gruesome. There was a hole in her eye socket, blood pouring. She was dying by the second.

"What happened?" Isis asked from behind him.

He couldn't take his eyes off Shamika. The body count around him was adding up. The guilt gripping him. When Isis saw the wound to her friend, she lost it.

"Aaaahhhh! Oh my God! Aaaahhhh!"

The screams snatched Dro from the guilt trip and he spun to face her. "Hey! Chill! Stop screaming. I need you to listen to me."

Isis's eyes were wide and she was hyperventilating, struggling to breathe.

"Ay! Isis!"

When she didn't respond, he slapped her. That got her attention.

"Listen. I need you to listen to me. The police about to come and I can't be here when they do. Take this gun and tell 'em you shot this nigga. Him and another nigga tried to run in here and you shot 'em. They gon' give you self-defense."

She looked at the gun like it was a snake. "Nah! I ain't touching that!"

42

"Listen, baby. You gotta trust me. You can do this. They gon' give you self-defense. You good. Just tell 'em you was defending yo'self. You bought the gun off the street and carry it for protection."

"Nah, I'm not doing it. I'm not finna go to jail." Then she began to cry. "Oh my God. I can't believe they shot my friend."

"Hey! You gotta listen. I'ma give you ten G's if you do what I say. You won't go to jail. Trust me."

She got defiant. "No. I'm not doing it. Oh, my God. I can't believe this just happened. I gotta call the police."

Not wanting to take a chance on her telling the police he killed somebody, Dro lifted the pistol to her face and squeezed the trigger.

Pop!

J-Blunt

CHAPTER 5

The Charger melted in the night, disappearing down side streets as Dro sped away from Shamika's house. "What the fuck?" he questioned. He shouldn't have popped Isis. His DNA was all over that house. In both females' pussies and throats. Saying the situation was fucked up was an understatement.

"What up, Dro?" Lunatic answered smoothly, sounding high as a kite.

"I think I fucked up, my nigga. I need to get this bitch-ass nigga Dirty. He just ran up on me at my bitch's house. Fucked her over."

There was a short pause. "You my nigga and I fuck with you. But I ain't tryna get in none of that shit, brah. That's on you."

Dro looked at the phone like it was Lunatic's face, mean mugging. "It's like that, my nigga? I tell you shit's fucked and that's how you respond? That shit with Tae really came between us?"

"Listen, brah. I'm all the way in Atlanta. If you need some paper or something, I got you. I just don't wanna get in no bullshit."

Dro chuckled, fully understanding Lunatic's position. He didn't respect it, but he had to accept it. "You got it, my nigga. Stay dangerous."

"Fa sho'. Savage."

Dro didn't have time to think about Lunatic's bullshit. He needed help getting out the jam he might've got in. So he called someone that could get answers.

"Young Dro, what it do playa?" the Hoe Whisperer answered.

"OG, I might be fucked. Shit popped off and I took care of my business. I might have to come see you. Can you hold me down?"

"You know I got you, baby boy. Come on down here to the ATL and kick it wit' me. My door always open for you. Just say when."

"I'm coming, Unc. But I need you to find Dirty for me. This nigga came at me. Tried to fuck me over."

Whisper understood the issue immediately. "Damn, nephew. If I was in town, I would be able to assist you. I didn't even know this, but my White Chocolate nigga was saying something about Monster having a little brother. He might be connected to all this shit.

Don't nobody know who Dirty is. He might be from out of town. But Nipsey don't like talking on the phones and shit. Paranoid-ass nigga. Gotta holla at him face to face."

"Who the fuck is Nipsey and white chocolate?"

"Nipsey is my nigga. I call him White Chocolate 'cause he a white boy. He plugged in the streets, but a super crazy-ass nigga. I think he got some bad dope and it fucked 'im up. But he know how to get that money. I'ma have somebody get in touch with him. Shouldn't take that long. I'ma set it up. I got you, nephew."

After ending the call, Dro concentrated on following all the laws of the road so he wouldn't have to go on a high speed chase. Fifteen minutes later, he pulled into the garage, hiding the Charger. His next couple moves were critical, and he was going to sit still until Whisper made the connect. Dirty had to go. That bitch-ass nigga didn't need to take another breath. And it only took Whisper two hours to hook everything up.

Dro was sleeping on the couch when he got the call. The number was unavailable.

"Hello?"

"This Dro?" a female asked.

He tried to place the voice, but couldn't. "Yeah. Who dis?"

"Nivea. Nipsey talked to your uncle and he wants to see you."

"A'ight. Where he at?"

The drive was only twenty minutes from Dro's house. The fucked-up part about it was the late hour. Two o'clock in the morning and he had to drive through downtown Milwaukee. If the police saw the young black man, he was getting pulled over for sure.

The Riverfront Condos were right on the Milwaukee River. Three hundred thousand dollar pads. Had to check a bag to live in the lofts. After finding a parking spot, he was buzzed in the building and took the stairs to the top floor. Nipsey's spot was at the end of the hall. Nivea answered the door.

"Hey, Dro." She smiled. "He's waiting on you."

The woman that answered the door was so fine that she should've been running around on the beach taking pictures in bathing suits. Guatemalan and Korean. Her tan skin looked flawless.

She was blessed with beauty and the slim build of a model. But Dro wasn't affected by her good looks. His baby momma was on the same level.

"What up?" He nodded, stepping into the palace. Shiny hardwood floors, twenty foot ceilings, and ten foot windows caught his attention. Expensive furniture. Big-ass flat screen TV above the fire lace. Rugs made out of fabrics the average person couldn't pronounce. Nipsey was living like a king.

"I'm Nivea. We talked on the phone. He's in the room. Come with me."

He followed the swaying of her small hips through the palace and to a door at the back. The room was just as plush as the rest of the house with couches imported from Italy.

Nipsey sat on the blue furniture, tall and lanky, skin tanned, hair slicked back, eyes dark with a hint of crazy. He wore a silk tank top, tailored white pants that rode high, showing black socks, and expensive hand-sewn shoes.

"What's poppin', my dude? Young Dro, right?" he asked, sounding like a nigga with white skin as he extended a hand. The pinky ring had a rock in it the size of an eraser top, glistening like a disco light.

"Yeah. Did Whisper holla at you?"

He reached for the black plate on the glass table. On it was an ounce of white cocaine. The crystals in the uncut dope shined like diamonds. "Yep. Come chill with me. Have a seat. You blow?" he offered.

"Nah. I'm good."

The pimp used a credit card to make up a line as big as a cigarette while he spoke. "I talked to somebody that knows yo' uncle. He said you needed my help. Holla at me," he said before picking up a straw and snorting the fat line.

"I need to find this nigga, Dirty. He was fuckin' with this nigga Eddie. You heard of them?"

Nipsey pinched his nostrils, taking several sniffs to clear his sinuses. "They said Eddie got killed at his own trap, right? Him and some workers. Triple body bags. You talking about him?"

Dro nodded. "Yeah."

Nipsey busted out into a high-pitched laughter. It sounded more like an animal shriek rather than a human sound. "You one of them Savages? Y'all knocked out Monster?" he asked, eyes wide and top lip twitching uncontrollably.

Dro shrugged, being non-committal.

The pimp shook his head, eyes popping, looking amused. "Ain't this some shit! I don't know if I should hug you or tell one of my girls to fuck you." He laughed before kicking his legs in the air and letting out another high-pitched shrill.

Dro could only watch him. It looked like he was celebrating.

"I know you think I'm crazy. And I am," he said, face serious, giving the crazy eyes. "They say the real crazy don't know they crazy, but that's bullshit. I do. I know the government implanting people with shit. Controlling people. They do it with the phones. That's why I don't touch 'em. Pay attention," he said before fixing another fat line. "That muthafucka Monster was a scumbag and de-served to die. Had all that money, but didn't like paying what he owed. Karma is a bitch. Y'all fucked the city up with that and did me a favor. Anything you need, you got it."

"I heard Monster had a brother."

Nipsey paused to snort the fat line. "Yeah, he do. Soft-ass muthafucka, name is Coupe. Li'l pussy that I should've been fucked up a long time ago. And Eddie was his boy. If Eddie connected to Dirty, than Coupe connected too. You ever heard of six degrees of separation? Everybody is connected. It's just a matter of knowing the right people that separate us. The whole world is connected like our bodies, man. Veins, arteries, organs. The planet is a living or-ganism. It's alive, my dude."

Dro nodded. "I hear you. Can you tell me about Coupe? Where he be at? You know where he live?"

Sniff. Sniff. "Nah. He live somewhere out of the city, I think. But he own a couple properties. Let me do some digging. I'ma get you everything you need to know real soon. I been waiting to meet you and we didn't even know it. I like ya energy, man. Real laid back kinda killa. I met a dude like you when I was in the feds. Bet you believe in God, too. If you didn't let the human need to believe in a higher power that don't exist hold you back, you would probably be a beast."

"I am a beast. God just keep me humble. If I wanna get in contact with you, how do I do that?"

Nipsey smiled at the response. "That was good shit, baby boy. I respect a real gangsta when I see one. Don't get in touch with me unless it's an emergency. Call Nivea. But I'ma call you as soon as I get that information. It won't take that long. I been up for two days and I probably won't sleep for two more."

***

The next day Dro took an Uber to the hospital to see his uncle. A week passed since Crush was shot and he was getting healthier every day. He started walking and looked like he was back to being his old self. He wasn't quite ready to leave the hospital, but it wouldn't be much longer.

When Dro walked in the room, Crush was lying in bed watching TV.

"Hey, nephew. What's going on, man?"

Dro sat down in the chair like his body couldn't handle all the bullshit and burdens he carried. "I think I fucked up, Unc."

Crush's eyes grew wide, forgetting about the TV. "What's up, nephew? What happened?"

"Dirty came to Shamika's house last night. Killed her. I got his nigga, but Dirty got away."

Crush's eyes reflected disbelief and anger. "Damn, nephew. I wish I coulda been there with you. Shit. So, what happened? Police come? You running?"

"Hell yeah. Because that ain't the worst part. I tried to get her friend to say she shot the nigga. She saw it. I offered ten G's, but she wouldn't do it. I couldn't let her tell on me, so I popped her. And my DNA all over that house. We just finished having a threesome right before they ran in the house. I think I'm fucked."

Devastation shown on Crush's face. "I don't even know what to say, man. How he find out where she live?"

"I don't know. But I'm looking for him. I talked to a crazy pimp last night and he knew Monster. Nigga got a brother. Coupe. He behind all this shit."

Crush sat up in bed, looking ready to put in work. "You need me? I'll check out this muthafucka right now. I'm s'posed to get discharged tomorrow, but fuck what them doctors talkin' about! Say the word, nephew."

"I can't let you do that, Unc. Just get better. You can't be running the streets and getting down if you ain't feeling all good. I'ma try to figure all this shit out. I don't plan being around Milwaukee too much longer. Its gettin too hot and I don't know how long I got 'til they come looking for me."

Crush simmered down. "Yeah, nephew. You probably have to run. You went to prison, so yo DNA is in the system. You might only got a couple weeks before they figure it out. Get a new phone. You gon' have to fall all the way back and stay off the social media."

"I don't fuck with that shit like that. That's how niggas catch cases."

"Good. So where you going? To North Dakota with Forever and the baby? You might be able to hide in one of them little towns."

"Nah. I'm in too much shit. I don't wanna bring nothing they way. I'ma go to Atlanta with Whisper for a minute to regroup and figure out how to move. If I can get these niggas before I leave, than I might go to Forever. But only if I get these bitch-ass niggas. I don't wanna put her life at risk again."

"That's real love right there. I know it gotta hurt staying away." Crush nodded, reflecting on what it felt like to be away from Candice. He had done the unthinkable to get her back.

"Not as much as seeing her laying on the ground bleeding. That shit fucked with me for a long time. I can't let that happen again."

CHAPTER 6

After leaving the hospital visit with Uncle Crush, he went back home to lay low. The charismatic televangelist, Bishop TD Jakes, was sweating profusely while he stomped around the stage. He was shouting at the top of his lungs and preaching the word of God like the Rapture was fifteen minutes away. His message was about getting back up when adversity knocked you down. Dro had watched the video at least twenty times and loved the motivation TD Jakes inspired. But today he was halfway listening, paying more attention to his phone, waiting for it to ring, awaiting the call from Nipsey. Ten hours had passed since he met the pimp and he was getting antsy. He felt like a sitting duck and didn't like it. The police were closing in on him and time was of the essence.

When the phone vibrated, a jolt of excitement shot through his body. His hopes were dashed when He checked the screen and saw it was a jail call.

"What up, Twenty?"

"Damn, nigga. Fuck wrong wit'chu? Why you sound all sad and shit?"

Dro let out a long breath. "Man, shit so fucked up out here for me, my nigga. I might end up in that bitch with you if I don't figure a way outta this bullshit."

"Damn, my nigga. I was calling with good news. What the fuck happened?"

"That bitch-ass nigga Dirty got at me. Shit so fucked up. I gotta find this nigga. You ain't gon' believe this, but that big fish we caught got a brother. I think he brought Dirty here. My nigga, it's so much shit I gotta tell you. Damn, I wish you was out here with me. Lunatic on some soft-ass shit and Unc still in the hospital. It's all on me. I'm fucked up, brah."

"No you ain't. You ain't gotta get at them niggas by yo'self. I just came from court, my nigga. They dropped them charges for those bodies. Brandon is a beast, my nigga! Got self-defense, but they keeping the charge of being a felon with a pistol. Hit me wit' that enhancer, so I'm facing fifteen years. My bail ten G's. It's already paid. Come get me! "

"Hell yeah!" Dro celebrated, happy to have his nigga back out with him. "I'm on my way right now. How long 'til they let you out?"

"Shit, I don't know. Just come get me, nigga. And bring some weed."

"A'ight. But I can't drive my car. I might be hot. You got one of those trappers I can use?"

"Yeah. Get at my li'l bitch, Bianca. Matter of fact, I'ma have her get at you. Stay dangerous."

"You know it. Savage."

Instead of driving downtown, Dro rode passenger in the blue Pontiac Sunfire, thankful for the tinted windows. He didn't want to be seen. Bianca took care of the driving. She was Twenty's main bitch. She stood just five foot tall with light skin and was thick in all the right places. Ass like whoa. Big titties. Pretty face. And she had a thing for colorful wigs. Today's choice was lime green. It matched her dress.

"Why y'all niggas so damn bad, Dro?"

He gave her a look. "I don't know what that mean. I ain't bad."

Bianca cut her eyes at him. "Didn't you just get shot a couple months ago? Twenty got shot. Lunatic got shot. Tae dead. Don't talk to me like I don't know y'all niggas. I love Twenty, thug, but damn. Gettin' shot and goin to jail is a lot. Why y'all so damn bad?"

"We just products of our environment. Only the strong survive out here. If we didn't wreck shit, somebody might think it's sweet. But we been tryna put that shit behind us. At least I have. Shit just been crazy."

"I wish you'd tell yo' friend to leave all that crazy shit behind him. This jail and gettin' shot shit fuckin wit' a bitch nerves."

Dro chuckled. "I think Twenty gon' stay the way he is forever. This street shit all that nigga knows."

"But you was the same way. You should tell him how to start a business like you did. I know he got the money. He don't buy nothing but guns and cars."

"What did he say when you talked him about it?"

"He don't wanna talk about it to me. But you like his brother, so he might listen to you. I just don't want my nigga to get fucked up."

Dro could hear the care and concern in her voice. Had heard the same tone in the voices of his mother, sisters, and Forever. "I'ma holla at him. I don't want my nigga to be fucked up either."

"So, if I do lose my man, you gon' take his place?"

Dro did a double take. "What you say?"

She turned to face him, looking him in the eyes. "I ain't no stupid bitch and I ain't no thot either. But Twenty's situation ain't looking too good. If I lose my nigga, I'm letting you know I wanna fuck with you. Twenty not my man, but my nigga. He know that if he ain't there when my pussy gets wet that I'ma get somebody to lick it. Since y'all boys and I know he would want me fuckin' a real nigga, I'm choosing you. I don't wanna creep around on him with you. But if it don't go right for my nigga, I want you."

Dro was a little surprised by her boldness. And even though she was pretty and had a phat ass, he didn't want to fuck somebody that his nigga fucked with. He wondered how Twenty would feel if he knew they had this conversation. "That shit is way too much, shorty. I don't fuck wit' my nigga's pieces. I don't do that. That's law, baby. I'm a real nigga and I don't get with that fuck shit. You cool, but I ain't tryna go there."

She nodded. "That's real shit. I respect a nigga that keep it real. I hope you don't look at me different. Like I said, I ain't no thot. I just wanted to let you know how I felt. And I would appreciate if you kept this between us."

Dro gave her a "yeah right" mug before shaking his head.

After parking out in front of the county jail, they sat to wait for Twenty to be released. They didn't have to wait long. Forty-five minutes later he stepped onto the sidewalk wearing a pair of Jordan's, dark jeans, and a white T-shirt, his dreadlocks swinging as he began looking around. Bianca bolted from the car like it was on fire, the hair on her lace front blowing in the wind as she booked it to her man.

"Hey, baby!" she yelled before jumping in his arms and tonguing him down.

Dro walked over after the lovers had their moment. "What it do, boy?" he asked as the brothers shared a hug.

"Damn, my nigga. It feels so fuckin' good to be out that bitch. Sixty-three long-ass bitch-ass days. Where the weed at?"

"In the car. C'mon nigga. Let's get the fuck from downtown. Being around all these police and jail shit making me nervous."

During the drive to Twenty's house, they didn't talk about the issues facing Dro. Bianca was present and they didn't want her to know what they did in the streets. Twenty was serious about sticking to the G-code.

When they got to his house, Dro waited in the living room while Twenty got some fresh outta jail pussy. Thirty minutes later he walked out of the room shirtless, wearing a pair of shorts and smoking a blunt. The smile on his face told of how happy he was to be able to fuck and smoke weed again.

"On what, that pussy don't have a nigga feeling like he really free?" Dro grinned.

"Pussy and a blunt. If we could smoke weed and get pussy in jail, it might not be that bad. I would definitely take Bianca in with me. Her head game is fire, my nigga."

Dro thought about the conversation he had with Bianca while they waited for Twenty's release. "You fuck wit' her tough, huh?"

"Yeah. That's my bitch. But I ain't saving her. You wanna see what that head game like?"

"Nah, I'm good," Dro declined. "She said some shit about fuckin' wit' me if somethin' happened to you."

Twenty didn't look surprised. "She said that shit before. It was a long time ago. She love fuckin' wit' real niggas and she know you my nigga. I don't give no fuck. I fuck wit' her, but she community property. But fuck that bitch. What's this shit about you finna go to jail, nigga? Fuck was that about?" he asked, flopping down in the couch.

"I think I fucked up this time. That nigga Dirty came to Shamika's house and tried to get me out the way. Ended up shooting

54

my bitch in the face, but I got the nigga that came with him. Dirty got up outta there. I tried to get Shamika's friend, Isis, to say she killed the nigga and say it was self-defense. Offered her ten G's, but she wouldn't take it. So I offed her ass. Left her on the floor next to Shamika and the other nigga."

Twenty nodded. "I might've did the same shit. Bitch was gon' tell. That shit was gangsta."

"But we had just finished fucking. Had a threesome and this nigga showed up right after. My nigga, my DNA all over that house and all over them hoes."

Twenty winced. "Damn, my nigga. That's fucked up. When this shit happen?"

"Last night. I talked to this white pimp that Whisper plugged me with and he sayin' Monster got a brotha that's connected to all this shit. Nigga named Coupe. The nigga Eddie that we left stankin' at the trap was his nigga. Nipsey working on gettin' me a location on Coupe."

"Damn, Dro. You been out here fuckin' it up. And as soon as you get that location, we riding down on them fuck niggas. I got a bullet wit' Dirty's name on it. Fag-ass nigga tried to get me bodied."

"I'm waiting. Hopefully we can get these niggas soon 'cause I'm burnin' up out this bitch. Whisper said he gon' hold me down for a li'l while. I tried to call Luna for some AA, but he on some bullshit. Said he ain't tryna get involved, but he would look out if I need some money. Fuck kinda shit is that? After all the shit we been through? I think he still salty 'bout that shit with Tae."

"Ain't no need to think. He salty 'bout that shit, brah," Twenty confirmed. "You clapped up bro and you lied about it. Shit, I told you how I felt. But you still my nigga. Lunatic still got love for you, but he prolly just need some time."

"Well, I'm going down there once we get these niggas. And we - " Dro paused when his phone began vibrating. "Nivea" shown on the screen. "This might be it right here," he said before answering. "Hello?"

"Hi, Dro. Nipsey wants to talk to you. Can you come over?"

***

"I'ma tell you right now," Dro warned as they climbed the stairs to the condo. "This nigga crazy as fuck. Thinks the government controlling us with cell phones and shit. Be saying all kinds of weird shit. But Whisper fucks with 'im and said he valid."

Twenty busted out laughing. "On what, he one of them aliens abducted me and stuck something up my ass type of niggas?"

Dro shook his head and laughed.

After being let into the loft by Nivea, they were escorted to the same room Dro met him in during the last meeting.

"Nipsey, this my nigga, Twenty. Twenty, this Nipsey," Dro introduced.

The pimp gave Twenty the once over. "You one of the Savages too?"

Twenty nodded. "Yeah."

The pimp leaned back and let out a high-pitched laugh.

"Man, what the fuck?" Twenty jumped.

"Chill, young go-rilla. This what I do, baby." Nipsey chuckled. "I was tellin' yo' boy, Dro, last time he was here that I'm fans of you dudes. Y'all did me a favor by gettin' Monster's bitch ass out the way. I couldn't stand that pussy-ass fart fuck. Y'all ever heard of James Baldwin?"

Dro and Twenty glanced at each other to see if one of them knew what the fuck Nipsey was talking about.

"I can see by y'all looks that neither one of y'all know who that is. Let me explain. James was a queer muthafucka and a good writer. Real famous amongst black scholars. Wrote about the issues facing black people and shit during the civil rights era. See, sometimes it's a struggle to achieve, reveal, and confirm human identity and human authority. Especially when muthafuckas don't understand the beautiful horror of life. But you know what I learned about sufferings? The muthafuckas that don't suffer don't grow or discover what they are. When a man is forced to snatch his manhood out the fire, he learns somethin' every time he makes a move. You know what I'm sayin'?"

Dro and Twenty gave one another questioning looks. "Man, what the fuck is you talking about?" Dro asked.

"I'm talking about the feds, homie. Them mu'fuckas crazy, yo. Can come and take yo' shit. I'm telling you brothas to be careful out there, man. Shit real. Just the other day a muthafucka stabbed theyself in the eye with they own metal straw. Bitch was sipping her drink and tripped. The fuckin' straw went through her eye and damn near killed her. Gotta be careful 'cause even the simple shit can kill you."

Twenty busted out laughing. "Is this a fuckin' joke, my nigga? What the fuck is goin' on? You got a hidden camera around this bitch?"

Nipsey sat up, his face hard, a serious look in his eyes. "It bet' not be a muthafuckin' camera in here! Nivea! Nivea! You got a muthafuckin' camera in my house? You know I don't play that shit!"

Dro and Twenty busted out laughing.

Nivea came to the room door. "What are you screaming for?"

Nipsey jumped up like he got struck in the ass by a lightning bolt. "You got a camera in here? You know I don't play that shit!"

She didn't look surprised by his antics. She stayed calm. "There are no cameras in the house, baby. I know they are used by the government to keep tabs on people. I know better, baby."

"God damn right, you better know better," he said before flopping back onto the couch. He grabbed the plate of cocaine that sat on the table in front of him and made a fat line. "Now like I was saying, I got the information you need, young Dro." He paused to take a big sniff of the dope.

Dro and Twenty looked at each other, both weirded out by the pimp.

"Yeah!" Sniff. Sniff. "You niggas wanna hit this bitch? Hoe gon' put somethin in yo' life to make you tell yo' bitch you ain't neva comin' back home."

"Nah, we good," Dro spoke up. "Why you call me over here? I thought you had some info for me."

Sniff. Sniff. "Yeah, I do, baby boy. I got that bitch, Coupe. Yeah, funky hoe got a studio on the north side, an auto detailing shop on the south side, and the bitch own some rental properties all over the city. I just need y'all to do one thing." He paused, giving them a serious look. "Make sure y'all kill that bitch!"

***

"What the fuck was that shit, my nigga?" Twenty asked as he and Dro walked towards the Camaro.

Dro shook his head. "I told you that nigga was crazy."

"Nah, brah. That nigga ain't crazy. That nigga insane! What the fuck was he talkin' 'bout with that crazy-ass story? Man, I don't neva wanna see that nigga again."

"Hopefully we won't have to. Let's go look at that studio and see if we can catch these bitch-ass niggas."

"Now you talkin' my language." Twenty smiled as they hopped in the sports car. "So who the fuck got down on Crush?"

"These bitch-ass Ride Out Boyz."

"I heard of them niggas. I thought they was gettin a li'l money. I didn't know they played with that fire."

"Me and Unc got down on one of them niggas. Chino. He used to fuck Unc over back when he was on that shit and we took his shit. Crush shot him too. Guess he ran up on Unc at the laundromat and tried to take him out."

"Damn. How many times Crush get plugged?"

"Caught six of 'em. But he good. Shamika helped me get down on them niggas. I crept through the bathroom window on they ass. I was fuckin' them niggas up, but couldn't get Chino. Popped him a couple times though."

"You wanna ride down on them niggas again to make sure his dick in the dirt?"

"Not really. I don't got time for that shit. I just wanna get Dirty and Coupe and get the fuck out the city."

"Say no more. But I'm bringing it to all them bitch-ass Ride Out Boyz if I see 'em. That's my word. Crush my nigga."

Dro and Twenty sat behind the tinted windows of the Camaro, parked half a block from Hit Makerz, the studio owned by Coupe.

58

They had been posted for hours, watching the comings and goings of the studio patrons. When the day changed to night, they walked up close to take a look around. The sign on the door said the spot closed at ten o'clock. They planned to wait until lock up and kidnap whoever closed up. They ended up having to wait until almost ten-thirty. That's when a tall skinny nigga with brushed waves stepped outside, using his key to lock the door. Before he could put the keys in his pocket, the Savages were on his ass.

"Unlock the door and go back in, nigga!" Twenty said, pressing the 40 to the back of his neck.

"We don't got no money in here, man. This just a studio," he stalled.

Dro slapped him in the face with the 9 milli. "Shut the fuck up and open the door, bitch-ass nigga! We gon' do the talkin'."

"Okay! Okay!" He winced before unlocking the door.

The Savages shoved him in the building, throwing him to the floor. The victim was terrified as he stared into their masked faces.

"Where Coupe at, nigga?" Twenty demanded.

"I-I don't know, brah. H-he don't be comin' through here like that."

Dro pointed the gun to his face. "Quit lyin', nigga. Tell me where he at before I blaze yo' bitch ass."

"C'mon, man. Please don't kill me. I don't know where he at. On my mama, I don't. I just run the studio. I ain't no hustler. I don't even play in the streets. Please, fam. I don't know shit."

Dro glanced at Twenty. They agreed that he was probably telling the truth.

"You gotta gimme somethin, nigga," Dro said. "Where he be at? That nigga owns a lot of shit."

"Okay, um, they spend a lot of time at the car shop. I think he got an office in there. But it's closed already. That's all I know."

"Who is that nigga Dirty? Where he from?" Twenty asked.

"Uh, he was - I mean, is – Eddie's cousin. Came from Minnesota. I don't know too much about him 'cause he just came around and I only seen him once or twice. That's all I know, brah. Please don't shoot me. I ain't gon' say nothing to nobody. I just wanna go home, brah. Please."

The bass from a loud stereo made everyone pause. Dro looked out the door and saw an aqua blue Benz parking at the curb. Twenty snatched the hostage up by his shirt, forcing him to look out the window.

"Whose car is that?"

"That's Levi car. She's part of Coupe team."

Dro smiled with his eyes. Twenty read the look and nodded. They finally got a break. She was going to tell them everything.

They watched from the window as the butch climbed from the driver's seat of the Benz. A thick, bad bitch hopped out the passenger side and they walked towards the studio. Dro got ready, pointing his gun at the door while Twenty kept an eye on their captive. Levi was walking upon the porch when the studio manager began screaming.

"Levi, don't come in here, they - "

Twenty reacted quickly shooting him in the head twice.

Pop, pop!

The screaming and shooting made Levi pause and pull a pistol. It was a Glock nine with a drum. She backed away from the door, moving towards her ride.

Not wanting to let her go, Dro ran outside, his nine barking like a dog.

Bocca, bocca, bocca, bocca, bocca, bocca!

Levi's girl began screaming.

The dyke didn't hesitate and returned fire.

Clap, clap, clap, clap, clap, clap, clap!

Dro took cover on the side of the building. Twenty peeked outside, using the door for a shield, and let his 40 off.

Pop, pop, pop, pop, pop, pop, pop!

Levi was trained to go and ducked out of the way. Then she turned her cannon loose, shooting up the studio and holding her own with the fifty shot drum. Dro tried to use Twenty's shooting as a distraction and creep up on the lesbian. She saw him coming and sent shots his way before moving behind another car. Every time they moved towards her, she fired enough shots so she could retreat again.

The shootout lasted almost five minutes before Dro and Twenty eventually gave up. They would have to score the kill another night.

J-Blunt

CHAPTER 7

Crush was excited to finally be allowed to leave the hospital. He stepped out of the bathroom, changing from the hospital gown into a button up polo, slacks, and loafers.

"You look handsome." Candice smiled, getting up from the bed to hug him.

He kissed her lips." Even on my best days, I don't got nothing on you, baby."

"That was a good one." She blushed.

"It was the truth. Have I told you how much I love you lately?"

"Yes. But it wouldn't hurt to hear it again."

"I'm still alive because of your love, baby. When I was laying on that laundromat floor bleeding, I kept thinking about you and Kathy. Whenever I thought about the bullets or the pain or dying, I could feel myself getting weak. But when I thought about my girls, it gave me strength. I'm alive because of your love, baby. Love is the most powerful force in the world. Not even death can prevail over true love. Ain't that amazing?"

Candice melted, tears filling her eyes. "Yes. Love is amazing. And so are you. And do you know what else is amazing?"

Crush stared into her sparkling eyes, trying to guess. "I don't know. What?"

"You taking me home and making love to me for the rest of the day. You've been in the hospital all this time and I missed you."

Crush slipped his hands down to her soft derrière and squeezed, his lips melting against Candice's in a passionate kiss. Then the room door opened. Nurse Maggie was rolling a wheelchair into the room.

"I'm sorry. I didn't mean to interrupt."

The love birds broke the embrace. "It's okay." Crush laughed, eyeing the papers in her hand. "Do you have the discharge papers?"

"Yes. I just need you to sign them and then you can be on your way. But you have to leave in this wheelchair. Hospital policy."

After putting his signature on the papers, Crush hopped in the wheelchair. Candice rolled him from the room and through the hospital. After an elevator ride to the lobby, they were headed towards the glass double doors.

Two black men approached. One was tall, bald, and wearing casual clothes. The other was short, with brushed waves, wearing designer jeans and a gold chain.

"Christopher Patrick?" the taller one asked, stopping in front of the wheelchair.

Crush frowned, eyeing the men suspiciously. "Yeah. Who are you?"

"I'm Detective Jackson and this is my partner, Detective Scott. We need to talk to you down at the station."

"What's going on? He got shot. He didn't do anything wrong," Candice defended Crush.

"This has nothing to do with him getting shot, lady," Scott spoke up. "Can you walk?"

"Yeah. If I'm not under arrest, then I don't want to go to the station. I'll answer the questions right now. What is this about?"

Jackson was losing his patience. "Listen, man. We don't want to do this in public, but if you insist, we will."

Crush matched his irritation. "I do insist. I know my rights. Matter of fact, I don't want to talk at all. Contact my lawyer. Let's go, baby."

Candice tried to maneuver the wheelchair around the detectives, but they each grabbed an armrest, holding it in place.

"Alright. We doin' this the hard way," Jackson said, pulling out handcuffs, roughly grabbing Crush's arm. "Christopher Patrick, you are under arrest for the murder of America Jones. Anything you say can and will be used against you in a court of law..."

"What are you doing?" Candice cried. "Why are you doing this to us? He didn't do anything. What are they talking about, Chris?"

"I don't know, baby. Call my nephew. Tell him what happened and to send me a lawyer!"

***

Crush sat in the holding cell going over in his mind how the fuck he got here. He was being arrested for America's murder - a murder he didn't even commit. How the hell was this happening? Had somebody fed the police bogus info? Was Dro locked up for it already and they were charging him with some kind of party to the crime? It didn't make sense.

Keys at the door snatched him from his thoughts. Jackson and Scott stood outside.

"Chris, come with us. We wanna talk to you," Scott said.

"Is this about my phone call? I don't want to talk without my lawyer present."

"Only way any of that is going to happen is if you come out of that room," Jackson nodded.

Crush followed them to the interrogation room. It was small with a table in the middle and three chairs around it. On the table was a tablet. After everyone had seats, Scott spoke up.

"Do you smoke? Wanna cigarette?"

"Nah. I don't smoke. When do I get my phone call?"

"Soon, man. Real soon. You wanna tell us how you got shot?"

"I was at work and somebody came in and shot me."

Jackson smirked. "Came and shot you while you were at work, huh? Shit sounds personal. You know who did it?"

"I thought that's what y'all got paid for."

The detectives shared a laugh.

"You a sarcastic nigga, huh?" Scott said.

Crush's face remained serious. "I wasn't being sarcastic. I thought I was stating the obvious."

"Well, it's not. We ain't the ones investigating your shooting. But we did see the footage. Nigga tried to put yo' ass on ice. What you know about the Ride Out Boyz?"

"Nothing."

Scott nodded. "Okay. What you know about the Savages?"

Crush didn't say a word.

"You don't got nothing to say?" Jackson asked.

"I wanna call my lawyer." Crush said firmly.

"You gonna get the call. We have to do that by law. We're just talking right now. Off the record. Nothing is being recorded. Do you know the Savages?"

"Never heard of them," Crush answered.

Jackson tapped the tablet screen and swiped a couple times. "You telling me you don't know them?"

On the screen were booking photos of Dro, Twenty, and Lunatic.

"The one on the right is my nephew. Y'all already know that. We got the same last names."

"Dro, right?" Scott nodded.

"Man, what do this got to do with me?" Crush asked, getting frustrated.

"A'ight, brah. We gonna cut the bullshit. We're about to charge you with a body. America. Dro's baby mama. But we don't want you. We want your nephew. If you tell us that he was behind America's murder and give us solid shit about Monster's murder, we're gonna forget we ever had this conversation. All charges dropped."

Crush visibly flinched. "I don't know none of this shit y'all talking about. I didn't kill America. I was at home with my wife and daughter."

Jackson swiped the tablet screen. A photo of a manila envelope showed. America's name was written on it.

"That your handwriting?"

Crush panicked on the inside, but his face remained unfazed. "I never seen that envelope."

"We got DNA on this envelope. It matches you. It won't be hard to match your handwriting. Even if you didn't do it, we got enough evidence to say that you did. It look like you bailed her out and killed her after she got off the phone with Dro asking for him to bail her out. We don't need more than that, Crush. All the phones calls are recorded. We were listening."

Crush's confidence broke a little. "I don't know about none of that shit you talking about. Let me get the phone so I can call my lawyer."

***

It was a sunny Saturday afternoon. Seventy-five degrees. Not a cloud in the sky. Perfect day to let the top down and turn the music up in your car.

But Dro didn't have sunny thoughts or care that it was Saturday as he pulled up to his parent's house. His heart was heavy from the conversation he needed to have with his stepfather. He walked in and saw his sisters sitting on the couch watching TV.

"Hey, Rupee," Kailah sang.

"Hey, brother." Shanice waved.

"What up, y'all. Where Pop at?"

"I think he upstairs with Mama."

Damn. He was hoping to avoid having to explain this to his moms. He didn't want to see the heartbreak in her eyes when she found out what he did in the streets. But it was necessary and had to be done. After climbing the stairs, he walked to the end of the hall. The door was open. Pop sat in bed watching TV. Mom lay next to him, a phone in hand.

"What up, y'all?" he nodded.

"Hey, baby." His mother smiled.

"Sup, young man?" Lenny nodded.

Dro walked in and leaned against the dresser. "I need to talk to y'all for a minute. And it's serious."

When Marcia noticed the look on her son's face, she became alarmed. "What's going on, Ruben? Is everything okay?"

He shook his head, letting out a deep breath. "Nah. I got a lot goin' on in my life and I don't know if I'ma make it out alright. I wanna turn my laundromats over to y'all. Use it to take care of everybody and my baby."

Both parents sat up, eyes wide with fear. Lenny spoke first. "What are you talking about, Ruben? You scaring me, man."

"Me too. What's going on? Somebody shooting at you again?" his mother asked.

He didn't want to answer the question. "I'm in a lot, y'all. I'm in the streets for real. Police might start looking for me real soon and I wanted to let y'all know before y'all seen it on the news."

"What do you mean, Ruben? What did you do to make the police want to look for you?" Marcia asked, the pain he didn't want to see showing in her eyes.

"Murder. Maybe."

Heartbreak and surprise washed across his parents' faces.

"Murder, Ruben!?" Marcia shrieked, her mouth open wide.

"Somebody tried to kill me. I shot back in self-defense and a couple people got killed."

His mother was lost for words and couldn't believe what she was hearing.

Lenny tried to think rationally. "If it's self-defense, then we can help. Do you need a lawyer?"

"Nah, Pop. I'm not taking this to court. They won't ever let me go. I don't wanna get old and have to spend the rest of my life in a cell. I'm leaving town and I wanna give y'all the businesses. I can't operate laundromats on the run. If they successful, y'all can pass 'em down. Start a chain."

"Why are you running if it was self-defense?" his mother asked.

Lenny answered. "They not gon give him a fair shake in court, baby. More than one person was killed. He's young and black."

Dro was surprised that his stepfather understood. "They gon' lock me up forever, Ma. I don't wanna go through that. I can't."

She began to cry. "Oh, my God. Lord Jesus, this is too much! How did you get into somethin like this?"

"I ain't a school kid. I'm in the streets. I been gettin' it how I live for as long as I can remember. That's how I got the laundromats. I was tryna get out. Then all this crazy stuff started happening."

"That's what happened at the State Fair?" Lenny asked.

Dro nodded, thinking about Asia.

"Oh my God!" Marcia cried. "Ruben, baby, what did you do? I knew you wasn't a saint, but I never imagined this. I don't even know what to think."

"I wanted to come tell y'all this so you would understand everything that's about to happen. I know y'all raised me better and I really tried to stop running the streets. I got baptized. Me and Forever made plans to settle down. When I found out she was pregnant, I thought God gave me everything back that I lost. Like Job. I didn't want none of this to happen, but this is how it is."

"I'ma pray for you, baby. It sounds like that's all I can do. If God kept you around this long after everything you've been through, than He can do it again," his mother said, gaining strength with the confidence of her faith. "We serve an amazing God. We still believe what the preacher said when you was little. God has a plan for your life."

Dro heard what she was saying, but didn't feel the words. He couldn't see far enough ahead to understand the plan God had for his life. Any plan the Maker had for him went down the drain when he shot Isis.

"I hope so, Mama. I don't wanna be here that much longer. I gotta stay away to keep everybody safe. Y'all might not near from me for a while, but I'll check in when I can."

Lenny nodded, getting up from the bed and wrapping Dro in a hug. After the embrace, they stared at one another, both men fighting back tears, refusing to let them spill.

"You take care of yourself, son. I'ma be praying for you, too."

"I will, Pop."

When his mother got up front the bed and hugged him, the sad look and tears on her face threatened to undo Dro's sanity.

"Take care of yourself, Ruben. I love you so much. I do. And God loves you too. Just call whenever you can so that we know you safe."

"I will. I promise I will, Ma."

"You know what would be good, Ruben?" his pop asked.

"What up?"

"If you came to church with us tomorrow. You in a real jam, son, and it looks like you might need some clarity or guidance. We might not be able to give you the advice or some of the answers you seek, but God can."

Dro thought about Lenny's words. The last place he wanted to go was to church. But what else did he have to lose? All his life God had been speaking to him through people and situations. And now that he appeared to be all out of answers, having one last encounter with God might not be a bad thing.

CHAPTER 8

Dro's heart felt heavy with sorrow. Talking to his parents was as emotionally draining as a funeral: his. And it would become his literal death if he didn't find a way out of the jam he was in. The only good news was him getting closer to Dirty and Coupe. He wished he could've got the dyke last night. but she was a soldier. If the opportunity came, he was going to blow her shit back. But the most important marks were Dirty and Coupe.

After leaving his parents', he stopped at the fish mart to get a salmon plate before heading home. He was about to get in the rented Altima when he saw the green Caravan pull into the parking lot. Deidra noticed him at the same time.

"Ruben!"

He paused, waiting for America's mother to get out of the van. He had always liked the sassy vet. She had a combination of street and class and America looked just like her. All the body and good looks were held by the mother first. At forty-four, she still turned the heads of most men, young and old.

"Hey, Deidra. How you doing?" Dro asked as they shared a warm embrace.

"I'm making it. Taking it one day at a time."

Her eyes reflected the truth in her words. In a matter of months she had lost her granddaughter and daughter. Every day was a struggle.

"That's all we can do."

"I want to thank you again for helping us with the funeral. You didn't have to do that."

"C'mon, Deidra. You don't gotta thank me for that. It was nothing. Even though me and America had our differences, I still loved her and would do anything to help her. I know that nigga Block did this. And if I catch him, it's a wrap."

"I thought it was Block, too. But I talked to some detectives and they said he died before she did. I think they gon' find who did it. The look in they eyes said more than they told me. I can read a man.

Especially a black man. They asked about you and said they wanted to talk. Did you talk to 'em yet?"

Dro's heart sank to the bottom of his feet. Even though she didn't say their names, he knew Jackson and Scott had paid the visit. And if they were investigating, they must've been looking at him as a suspect. America had tried to set him up. It was real. Now their snitch was gone and they were coming after him.

"Nah, I didn't talk to 'em yet. Do you know they names? I can call 'em and see what they want. Did they leave you a card?"

A light went on in her head. "They sho' did," she said before reaching into the van's center console. After a little digging, she pulled out a business card. It had Detective Jackson's number on it. Dro put the number in his phone and gave it back.

"Okay. I'ma call soon as I get home. Let me get this fish to my mother's crib before she go crazy."

"I'm about to get me some, too. It was good seeing you. Take care of yourself. And tell your mother I said hi."

"I will. Take care."

The sounds of ankle chains dragging on the ground played in Dro's ears as he drove home. Damn. That net around him was getting tighter. Jackson and Scott were becoming pains in the ass. Every time he turned around, they were fucking with him. Now they wanted to talk to him about America. He needed to get rid of Dirty and Coupe tonight so he could get the fuck out of Milwaukee.

He had just pulled in the driveway when he spotted his neighbor checking the mail.

"What up, Ronnie?" Dro nodded as he climbed from the rental car.

"I'm good. What up with you?"

"I can't complain."

"Ay, the police just left about two minutes ago. They came and knocked on our door and asked questions about you."

Dro froze, a chill vibrating his body. "What they look like?"

"A brotha. Kinda short. Brushed waves. Gold chain. Said his name was Detective Scott. I didn't believe he was really a detective until he showed me a badge."

Dro checked his surroundings as he walked over to get more information. "What he ask? What did you say?"

"When was the last time I seen you? How often you at home? The kind of car you drive?"

"And what did you tell him?"

Ronnie smiled. "I lied. Told them you drove a grey F-150. And that I ain't seen you in a couple days."

Dro gave him a handshake. "Good shit, my nigga. You a good dude. You take it easy and take care of that family."

Dro left his house, knowing he could never return. Fuck. The net was wrapped around his neck and cutting off his oxygen. Time was running out. Jackson and Scott were on his ass. All of his moves would have to be measured. One slip could put him in a casket or cell.

He drove cautiously away from home, heading for Twenty's house. His eyes searched everything, on the lookout for any police cars and avoiding busy streets. When the phone rang, he put it on speaker.

"Yeah."

"Ruben, this is your aunty. They took Crush," Candice cried.

A sharp pain hit Dro's heart. "Who took him? When?"

"This morning when we were leaving the hospital. The police took him. Two black men. Said they charging him with killing America."

Dro shook his head. "This shit crazy. Okay. I'ma take care of it and send him a lawyer."

"What is going on, Ruben? Did he kill you daughter's mother?"

"Nah. It gotta be some kind of mistake. That's why I'ma get him a lawyer. I'm about to get a new phone. I'll call you and get you the number."

"Wait, don't hang up. Can you give me some answers? You know why this is happening. Tell me."

He could hear the earnest concern in her voice and knew she was desperate. And it pained him that he wouldn't be able to answer her questions.

"I'm sorry, Aunty. I don't know nothing. This is something you gotta talk to Crush about. I gotta go so I can call the lawyer. Let me know if you need anything when I call back."

He hung up before she could say another word. Then he called Brandon.

"Hey, Ruben. What's going on, brotha?"

"My uncle got arrested this morning. Christopher Patrick. My aunty said they charging him with killing my baby momma."

"Shit. Okay. I'll go downtown and see what I can do. Do you know if he already has a lawyer?"

"Nah, I don't think so. I just got off the phone with my aunty and she didn't say nothing about it when I told her I would get him one."

"Okay. I'll get down there within the hour."

"And I need you to look into why they sweating me. Jackson and Scott came by my house and talked to my neighbors. I wasn't home, but they asked about me. I seen America's mother a little while ago and she said they were asking her about me too."

"Okay. Listen. I'ma probably need to see you. It sounds like you might have some trouble on your hands. Can you come to the office Monday? I'm gonna need a couple days to figure all this out."

"I'ma try to hang around. I'm in a lot of shit. I'm leaving town after I take care of somethin'. But if I'm here on Monday, I'm coming to yo' office. Late afternoon. I'll text you before I come."

***

"Crush got locked up for America's murder," Dro told Twenty when he climbed in the passenger seat.

The dreadlock-wearing goon's eyes grew wide. "On what?"

"On everythang I love. I found out a li'l while ago when my aunty called. I sent Brandon to see what's goin' on."

"Damn, Dro. It's about time for you to go, brah. Only a matter of time before they be looking for you. How the fuck they know Crush had something to do with it? I thought you did it."

"I did. But I gave Crush the money to give her mama. I don't know how they connected him to this shit. He left it in her mailbox. Scott came looking for me. Talked to my neighbor. And I seen America's momma this morning. She said they looking for me too. I tried to tell her the nigga Block killed America, but they told her he died before she did. They gon' try to put all this shit on me."

Twenty lay back in the seat and shook his head. "This shit sound fucked up, brah. You wanna knock them bitch-ass fags out the way?"

Dro thought about the question. He had never even considered killing the pigs. But now that Twenty had mentioned it, knocking them out the box might not be a bad idea. They were trying to take his freedom. Getting rid of them would give him more time to get away. Might even hold up the investigation on him and his uncle.

"Yeah. We might have to look into that. They information public record. We can find them."

Twenty smiled, pulling the 40 from his pants. "I love to get my shit dirty. We on they ass. Now let's mob over to this car shop. See if Dirty n'em hoe asses there and knock they shit off.

***

Levi stood in the office of Flex-n-Shine, an auto detailing shop that was used as a front for handling business. She was mugging the nigga that sat in the chair behind the desk. She hated Trill's bitch ass, wanted him dead as bad as she wanted some pussy tonight. He was arrogant and took over the heroin game after Monster got killed. They had been partners. Monster and Trill were boys since way back. But unlike Monster's flashy style, Trill was cool staying in the background. When Monster died, he became more assertive and assumed total control of how the clique made moves. Levi didn't respect his slot.

"I ain't feeling how you all of a sudden get to call all the shots without talking to nobody. You raising the price by twenty percent. That's gon' hurt our buyers. We made our way 'cause we kept the numbers lower than everybody in the city. Raising 'em gon' make us lose money," Levi argued.

Trill didn't look concerned by her words. The dark-skinned chubby nigga sat back, looking calm as ever. "We gotta pay bills, shawty. Niggas catching cases and need lawyers and bail money. Shit ain't free and money don't come just because you want it or need it. This what gotta be done. I don't wanna do it, but we got to. We gon' drop the price in a minute. But for now, this how it is."

"You know, we never had these money shortage problems when Monster was alive. If we not paying more to get 'em, then we shouldn't be charging more."

Trill mugged her. "Fuck is you tryna say?"

The lesbian didn't back down. "That this shit don't sound right. I think you should let some of us speak up. I know the game. I been down wit' the squad since day one. I think I earned the right to speak my mind and be heard."

"And you wanna know what I think?" Trill mugged. "That you overstepping. You not my boss, nigga. I'm yours. Me and Monster was partners, not me and you. Not me and Coupe. I run shit now. Everybody that's down with what we doin' gon' do what I say do. If I need some advice, I'll ask. 'Til then, follow orders, soldier. Raise the prices. And my next order is for you to get out my office. You need to be finding who hit the studio last night. Do you know anything yet?"

Levi wanted to argue but it would be a waste of time. She wouldn't win. No one wanted to stand with her. So she humbled herself. "Nah. We got 'em on tape but they wore masks and gloves."

"Well, get yo' 'bout it 'bout it ass back out there and take care of that. We can't have niggas thinking that we sweet."

Levi left the office in a huff, pissed that Trill got absolute power. He was taking and spending more money. That was the reason for the raised prices. But nobody wanted to call him on it.

"You good?" Tommy Gunz asked when he saw the look on her face. He had been waiting for her in the lobby. Because of what happened last night, she was keeping a shooter with her at all times.

"Hell nah. Let's get the fuck up outta here. Trill on some power trippin' shit."

They stepped out into the late autumn night, walking across the dark parking lot.

"What he say?" Gunz asked.

"Raising the numbers to a hundred a gram. That's gon' make us lose. Niggas got the low out there. Seventy-five a gram on the East side. Trill fucking up the business."

"He is the boss, ain't he?"

Levi stopped at the passenger door of the Toyota Corolla, mugging him. "He made hisself the boss because don't nobody wanna stand up to him, and that's the way he want it. That nigga taking more money. The prices not going up from the connect. He doing that because he taking more off top. That shit bogus."

"Can you prove it? If you can, holla at Coupe. He might speak up and try to do somethin'."

"Hell nah. Coupe's soft ass won't do shit. He the one that let Trill take over. When er'body seen that Monster's brother didn't say nothing, they just rode with it."

"Well, ain't shit you can do about it. Just keep stackin' yo' paper and doin' yo' own thang."

"Yeah. That's all I can do. C'mon. Get in so you can take me by this hoe's house. I need to eat some pussy to make me feel better."

When the navy blue Corolla pulled out of the lot, the Altima with the killers inside pulled out behind. Dro made sure to keep a half block's distance between the cars. The Savages watched, waiting for their moment to strike.

The opportunity came after twenty minutes of tailing. Tommy Gunz pulled up to a house on the North side and parked. Dro cruised up to the driver's side, Twenty hanging his pistol out the window.

Pop, pop, pop, pop, pop, pop!

Tommy Gunz didn't even know what hit him. The 40 caliber bullets tore into the side of his face and ear, blood and brain gushing from his head. Levi caught one of the bullets in the rib, making her cringe. She reached for the pistol in her waist, but was slowed by her painful ribs. By the time she got ahold of her shit, Twenty was pointing the 40 in her face.

"Put it down, bitch!"

She wouldn't drop the pistol, but she didn't make a move to lift it from her lap. He had the drop on her and if she flinched, it was over. Dro got out of the car, his pistol pointed at Levi. He opened the driver door and snatched Tommy Gunz from the car. Then he took Levi's pistol.

"Where Dirty?"

"Fuck you, nigga." She mugged, holding her side in pain.

Dro slapped her with the tool. "Bitch, I ain't playin'. Where the fuck Dirty and Coupe? Dirty ain't even from here. Don't die over a nigga you don't even know."

She smiled, showing bloody teeth. "I'd rather die a real nigga than live like a bitch-ass nigga. A coward dies a thousand deaths. A soldier dies once."

Dro respected her gangsta and knew she wasn't going to betray her niggas. She lived by the code. And died by it. He lifted the pistol to her face.

Pop, pop, pop!

CHAPTER 9

America's head bobbed up and down in Dro's lap. His hand guided her rapidly-moving head as she sucked him like a professional head giver. Then her mouth moved to his balls, sucking and humming. Her oral game had Dro in head heaven. He closed his eyes, focusing on the pleasure his baby mama was giving. And that's when he realized his baby mama was dead. His eyes shot open, looking down. America was staring up at him, blood dripping from the hole in her forehead.

"What the fuck?" he cursed, startling awake. He was relieved to discover that he had dreamed of America. But the head was real. Bianca was kneeling on the living room floor, chewing on his dick like it was the best thing she ever tasted. Twenty's words about her having good head came to mind. Shit was an understatement. That's when he realized he was getting head from his boy's girl. He grabbed her head to stop her.

"What the fuck you doing?"

"I'm getting you ready," she said, lust glazing eyes.

"Fuck is you talkin' 'bout?"

"This threesome, nigga," Twenty said from a couch across the room. He was already naked, watching.

Dro's face twisted as he scratched his head. "Man, what kinda freaky shit y'all on?"

"My bitch wanna fuck you, nigga. I told her to go 'head." Twenty said nonchalantly. "If you want her to stop, tell her. Otherwise, let's get it crackin'."

Dro looked down at Bianca. She was still kneeling on the floor, holding his dick.

"You want me to stop?"

The head was so good that he wasn't going to let her move until she drained the snake. "Hell nah. Do yo' thang."

Bianca got back to business, using her hand to stroke him while she sucked the head. When she went to deep throat him, shit made his toes curl. Twenty watched for a little while before walking over and joining the action. He knelt down and entered her from behind.

Bianca felt like a sex goddess as she used her body to satisfy the men. After a few minutes, they changed positions. She sat up to ride Dro while Twenty stood in front of her getting his dick sucked. Her pussy was good. Hot and wet. And she knew how to squeeze her pussy muscles. She had Dro ready to bust.

"Ayy, I'm finna nut," he warned, just in case she wasn't on birth control.

Bianca leapt up and started sucking him again. Twenty got back behind her and fucked her some more. When Dro's nut came, she drained him, swallowing it all and sucking him to make sure he was still hard.

"Now come get it from the back, nigga." Bianca said, kneeling on the floor.

Dro climbed behind her big brown ass and began drilling her while Twenty knelt in front of her getting chewed. The men had their way with the seductress until all were satisfied. Then they lay back and got high.

"Why you tell him what we talked about in the car? I told you not to say nothing, Dro," Bianca said as she lay on the couch rubbing her pussy.

"'Cause that's my nigga. I was s'posed to tell him. I would be a fake-ass nigga if I didn't."

"Savage life, baby." Twenty laughed, blowing out a cloud of smoke. "He was s'posed to tell me. That's my nigga. Real Friends by Boosie. Listen to it."

"It don't matter," Bianca said. "I got what I wanted anyway. This my first threesome wit' two niggas and I liked it. I want one in my ass and one in my pussy at the same time. Y'all down?"

"Hell, nah!" both Savages said at the same time.

"My dick ain't finna be that close to anotha nigga's. I don't care who he is. Fuck that!" Twenty said matter-of-factly.

"You trippin' wit' that shit," Dro added. "We real niggas, not weirdos."

"Damn." Bianca smacked her lips. "You niggas sho' know how to kill a bitch's vibe."

"Good. Because you vibing way too mu'fuckin' hard in this bitch," Twenty said.

***

Birds chirping outside made Dro reach for the phone. It was 7:14 a.m. "Ayy, I need to use yo' car, brah."

"You got it, my nigga. Where you going?" Twenty asked.

"Told Pop I was gon' go to church with the fam today."

Twenty looked amused. "On what, you finna go to church after we just fucked shit up last night?"

"I need some clarity, my nigga. What better place to get it than in the presence of God? On them old school gangsta movies, the mobsters always went to the Catholic Church for confessional."

"I guess it makes sense. But that shit too much for me."

"I never met a street nigga that went to church," Bianca said.

"Yes, you did. You looking at him. I fuck wit' God the long way. I ain't ashamed of what I believe in."

"My sister be on that same religious shit. That be too much for me sometimes. Be having me feeling all guilty and shit."

"That's conviction. Know you doing something wrong. That's a good thing to have. Shows that you still got a conscience."

"I don't feel bad about nothing I do," Twenty said. "So that mean I'ma psychopath, huh?"

***

Dro parked in the lot of First Assembly Church, wrestling with thoughts of turning the car around and bailing. The last time he went to church while he was heavy in the street life, he ended up getting shot and going to jail. That was the beginning of the bullshit with Jackson and Scott. And if that was a sign of things to come, he didn't want any parts of the church. He wasn't into playing with or pissing God off. Plus, he was still a little high from the blunts he had smoked with Twenty and Bianca. He had never been to church high and didn't want to start now. But he did tell his parents that he would be there. And the last thing he wanted to do was lie to his family.

"Gimme a sign, God," he prayed aloud as he contemplated leaving.

Then his phone rang. It was Forever.

He looked towards the sky. "For real, man?" he asked the heavens as he answered. "Hey, baby."

"I got your message about the new phone. What happened to the old one?"

"I had to get rid of it. Things is crazy out here and I needed to get a phone that no one had the number for."

There was worry in her voice. "I don't like the way you sound. Are you okay?"

He let out a breath. "Nah, I'm not okay, baby. But it ain't nothing you can do about it. I turned the laundromats over to my parents and told them to use it to help you and the baby. I'm leaving town. The police looking for me."

She sounded devastated. "No, Ruben! What happened?"

"You know what I do. I fucked up, baby. I don't know how much longer I got."

Forever didn't speak for a moment. She just cried.

Hearing her pain burned in Dro's chest. "I'm sorry, baby. I didn't mean for none of this to happen. You know I wanted to be with you and the baby. I was trying."

"No, Ruben! No! You should've stopped when I told you. Why couldn't you just give it to God? What am I supposed to tell our son?"

Hearing that he was having a boy made him feel good and bad. He always wanted a junior. But now it didn't seem like he would be able to raise him.

"It's a boy?"

"Yes."

"I don't know how I'ma do it, but I'ma figure a way out of this. I'm coming to you and my son when I put all this shit behind me. I just need time to figure it out."

"You keep telling me that, but it hasn't happened yet. I want to believe you. I want you here with us, but you keep getting deeper in the stuff you're in. Now you're wanted by the police. I don't know what to think or believe."

"Just don't stop believing that I love you and the baby. No matter what happens, just know that my love for my family is real."

Forever became quiet again. Dro waited.

"Where are you going when you leave Milwaukee?"

He wanted to tell her, but couldn't. "I can't tell you that. They might pay you a visit and I don't want you to get in trouble for lying to the police. Just know that I'ma get at you when I can."

"Where are you now?"

He chuckled. "Outside my parents' church deciding if I should go in. I asked God for a sign. And then you called."

"Go in, baby. God might have something that you need to hear. He is still answering your prayers. Go inside."

After the call with Forever, Dro decided to honor the word he'd given to his family and attend the service. Nostalgia hit him in the face as soon as he stepped through the front doors of the place he'd grown up worshipping in. The building had some upgrades, but it smelled and felt the same. He could hear the choir singing as he made his way into the building and through the sanctuary doors. The church could seat five hundred people and all the seats looked to be filled. People had their hands lifted to the sky, eyes closed as they sang along with the choir and worshipped. He paused to look around for his family and was greeted by an usher.

"Right this way, brotha," the tall, light-skinned man said.

"Clarence?" Dro asked, studying the man's face.

The usher paused to look at Dro. "Ruben, is that you, man?"

"Yeah, this me. What up, man? You still here?"

"Oh, snap! What's good, boy?" Clarence asked, hugging Dro.

"Yeah, I'm still here. Where you been?"

They hadn't seen each other since the last time Dro came to church with his family. That was ten years ago.

"I been out in that world. Just came to be with the fam. Where they at?"

He pointed to a spot in the third row. "They in the same spot they been in for years. It was good seeing you, brotha. Let's catch up when the service is over."

"You got it, brah. It was good seeing you, too," Dro said before making his way down to the aisle. He got lots of looks from church members he hadn't seen in a decade.

"Hey, son!" Lenny smiled, embracing Dro like he was seeing him for the last time.

"Hey, Pop."

"Glad you made it, baby. I thought you wasn't gon' show up," his mother said, giving him a hug similar to the one given by his stepfather.

"I wasn't gon' miss this for nothing in the world. Is Pastor Dane here today?"

Lenny pointed to the front of the church. "There he go. I think you gon' be in for a treat."

"Hey, Rupee. What you doing here? Ain't you gon' catch on fire?" Kailah teased as they hugged.

"Only witches catch on fire. Why you ain't burn up yet?"

She stuck out her tongue. "Shut up, ugly."

"Hey, brother." Shanice smiled as they hugged. "I'm glad to see you here. Hope this ain't the last time."

After greeting his family Dro sat down to listen to the choir. The deacon followed with a prayer. Then he turned it over to the man that would bring the word of God, the anointed Pastor Jeremiah Dane. He was a small man, standing only 5'4", with a slim build. He wore a dark suit, was bald-headed, and clean-shaven. Although he was short, his height never came into question when he stood in the pulpit and delivered the word of God. And as soon as he opened his mouth, Dro knew he was in for a treat. Five minutes into the sermon and he could feel the preacher's words tugging at his spirit.

"Just because you don't understand the path you're on doesn't mean God isn't leading you. Following God will take you through some stuff. Look at the children of Israel. God led them on a journey through the wilderness that took forty years. Most of them that started on the journey didn't make it to the Promised Land. And most of the people that made it to the Promised Land had no idea where they were going. They just trusted in the pillar by day and fire by night. And that's what we have to do, church. Somebody say, amen!"

"Amen!" the church erupted.

"Life is lived in the Valley and celebrated on the mountain top." He paused to let his words sink in. "Some of y'all are asking what I mean. Let me tell you. You have to go through something to get to something. You have to walk through the valley to get to the mountain top. And it won't always be pretty in the valley. And you won't always make the right decisions. And you might lose some friends along the way. You might get your heart broken. You might feel like you're going crazy. You might lose hope. You might get mad at God and curse Him. Some people you love might die. You might lose a child. You might feel like trouble is camped around you on every side. You might have come here this morning looking for a word from God on what your next move should be. And I'ma tell you what you should do. Follow God. Go where he tells you to go and do what he tells you to do. Trust him. When you hear that still small voice telling you that your season is up, walk away. Walk through the valley of the shadow of death so you can get to your mountain top!"

***

Dro was lost in thought about the service as he pulled up to Twenty's house. Everything the preacher said felt like it was for him. He had lost so much: friends, lovers, a child, money. Then he got it all back. Now he was about to run to places and had no idea where they would lead. It was a lot to take in. But he was going to take it as a sign and follow his gut.

He was climbing out of Twenty's Camaro when he locked eyes with the driver of a blue KIA. The blue sedan pulled in front of the Camaro and parked. He stepped upon the sidewalk watching as the woman climbed from the driver's seat. She was bad: short and thick, blonde dyed hair that came to her shoulders, pretty face with juicy lips that shined from gloss. She wore a T-shirt with "Got Jesus" on the front, a pair of white jeans, and heels. She followed him towards Twenty's house.

"Do I know you?" she asked.

"Shit, I could ask you the same thing. You following me."

"My sister is in that house. I came to pick her up."

Dro waited for her to catch up. "Bianca yo sister?"

"Yeah. How you know my sister?"

"Twenty is like my brother. My name is - " He paused, thinking about her "Got Jesus" shirt and how Forever reacted when he told her his name was Dro. "My name is Ruben."

"Hi, Ruben. I'm Lana. Now you wanna knock on the door or are we gonna stand here and talk all afternoon?"

He smiled. "Actually, I don't mind talking to you all afternoon. I just came from church and got the whole rest of the day to chill."

She laughed. "You Twenty's brother and you go to church? Yeah, right. Twenty is a street nigga."

"Don't judge a book by its cover. Just like you wearing a Got Jesus shirt and callin' niggas niggas."

"Don't be callin' me out, man." She laughed again. "I'm what they call a cursing Christian. Sometimes my mouth gets the best of me, but I love God."

Dro liked her. And despite everything going on in his life, he had to have her. "I'm a weed-smoking Christian, so don't think I'm judging you. That's what grace and mercy for, right?"

She looked surprised that he knew church lingo. "Okay, man. I see you for real about going to church. Wait, can you knock on the door so my sister knows I'm here? We out here kicking it and I almost forgot why I came."

Dro gave a couple taps before turning back to Lana. "I think you should leave her here, and me and you should get to know each other better."

She gave a flirty smile. "I hope you don't think I'm that easy, man. It takes more than a handsome face and church words to get me alone."

"Who dat?" Twenty called from inside the house.

"Dro."

"Dro? That's the weed-smoking Christian's nickname, huh?" Lana asked.

The door opened before he could answer. Twenty wasn't wearing a shirt and held a pistol in one hand. "How was church, saint?" He laughed. "What up, Lana? Bianca, yo' sister here!"

"Watch out, man." Dro chuckled, stepping into the house.

The nympho got up from the couch, smiling. "Ooh, did y'all meet? Sis, this is Dro. Dro, this is my sister."

"I met the weed-smoking Christian. Now grab yo' stuff and c'mon. I gotta get Brian, too."

"Don't you think he handsome, sister? And he a good nigga."

Lana cut her eyes at her sister. "Stop tryna play match maker and come on. I got stuff to do."

"I'm just tryna help you get the spiderwebs off that pussy, girl," Bianca cracked.

"Don't worry about my pussy. You either, Dro."

CHAPTER 10

The next morning Dro was awakened by his phone vibrating on the living room table. It was his lawyer.

"What's up, Brandon?" He answered groggily.

"Hey, Ruben. I just came back from court with Chris. Can you meet with me? We need to talk."

"Um, yeah. Gimme like thirty minutes. You in yo' office?"

"Yeah. I wouldn't drive if I were you. Take an Uber."

After ending the call, Dro called an Uber before going to freshen up. During the ride to the office, he kept playing the brief conversation he had with Brandon in his head. It sounded serious. He didn't even want Dro to drive. Damn. When he got to the law firm, he was allowed right into Brandon's office.

"Good morning, man. Have a seat. How are you?"

"I'm good. What you got?"

"This is serious, brother. I need you to listen. Jackson and Scott are looking for you in connection to America's murder."

Dro felt like he had been punched in the chest. "What? How? They finna charge me?"

"No. Your uncle has already been charged, though. I went to his arraignment this morning. I don't have all the evidence yet, but it looks like they have his DNA on the envelope that her mother gave the detectives. Apparently there was twenty-five thousand dollars in it and she used the money to bail her daughter out. Later that night she was killed. I don't think they can connect you to the shooting, but it's not looking good for Chris. They have evidence. Haven't released a possible motive yet, but I'll get it with the discovery. They may just want to talk to you because there isn't a warrant. Yet."

Dro closed his eyes, letting out a deep breath as he lay back in the seat. Crush was fucked and it was his fault. "Fuck. Okay. Did he get a bail?"

"Yeah. It's a hundred thousand right now. I'll see if I can get it lowered next week. Right now I think they're trying to squeeze him because I really think they want you. I did some digging and checked with a source and they're also trying to connect you to

Monster's murder. They have those nicknames and they figured out you're Dro. That's why I said 'yet' about the warrant. They're going to come for you. It's just a matter of when."

Dro was speechless for a moment. Shit was getting deep. Jackson and Scott had him by the nuts. They had everything they needed to run him down. But they hadn't come yet. And he wasn't sure why. "Damn, man. It sounds like I'm fucked."

"I wouldn't say that. Yet. I'm not sure how much evidence they have to connect you to everything. Can anyone connect you to America's murder?"

"Nah. Just Crush."

"So, you didn't say anything to anybody?"

"Nah."

"What about Monster? Did you talk to anybody about it?"

"Nah. I'm in the streets and I don't talk how I walk. But it is something else that's about to come out. My DNA is all over Shamika's and her friend's body."

Brandon frowned. "What are you talking about?"

"Shamika got killed about a week ago. That nigga Dirty tried to off me and shot her. I shot the nigga he was with and Shamika's friend. I tried to get her to tell the police she killed the nigga. She would've got self-defense. But she said no. So, to keep her from telling on me, I shot her."

Brandon shook his head. "Shit, Ruben. Damn, you are keeping me busy. You shouldn't have killed her, man. You might've been facing another felon with a gun charge, but not murder. You probably would've gotten self-defense for killing the guy that came at you, especially if your girlfriend got killed. So, how can you get connected to this? Why is your DNA an issue?"

"Because we just finished having a threesome right before them niggas ran in the house."

Brandon couldn't hide the disbelief. "So, you killed her right after you had sex with her?"

"Yeah. I felt like I didn't have a choice. I didn't want to go to jail."

Brandon was speechless for a moment. "Shit, dawg. You're ruthless. Okay. I'll try to get ahead of this, but it won't be easy with your DNA being in both women. Once the coroner figures out there was sexual contact and DNA, they'll send it to the crime lab. Only takes a week or two to get the results. Don't be surprised if Jackson and Scott come with that warrant soon."

"Yeah. That's what I'm thinking."

"So, how do you want to handle this? You want to turn yourself in and face the music?"

Dro mugged him. "Hell, nah! They gon' have to catch me. I know that with all the shit I'm in, they won't never let me out. Three separate homicides got my name on 'em. I'm about to have a son. I can't let 'em take me."

"Well, you should probably get a head start. And it wouldn't hurt to drop some money for these fees for you and your uncle. I'll cut you a good deal. I'll handle your uncle's case and yours, if and when you are caught, for one hundred thousand. How does that sound?"

Dro nodded. "I'ma see if I can get that to you before the night is up."

*****

"Hey!" Nivea smiled as she opened the door.

"Sup, Nivea? Where my boy at?" Dro asked as he walked into the plush pad.

"He's taking care of something in the other room. But he knows you were coming over. You can chill and wait for him. It might be a while. Would you like me to keep you company?"

Her offer caught him a little off guard. He searched the Korean and Guatemalan woman's pretty brown eyes for a hidden message in her words. She looked innocent.

"Yeah. Let's do it."

They walked into the room he met Nipsey in. Instead of sitting across from him, she sat next to him.

"Can I do anything to make you comfortable?"

He searched her face again, not understanding if she was trying be sexual.

"What that mean?"

She smiled, showing perfect teeth. "Whatever you want it to mean. At the moment, you're my guest and I want you to be comfortable."

"You mean sexual?"

"If that's what you want. But we can't do it here. You would have to come to my room."

He thought about the offer. Nivea was bad. She had a little frame. Average height. Small breasts and little ass hidden by the silk Versace dress. "Do I gotta pay?"

She laughed. "Of course you do. One thousand dollars an hour."

He almost choked. "Fuck you just say?"

"You can't put a price on a good time."

"Yes, I can. Ain't no pussy that good. I'm straight."

"You're not paying for sex, but the experience. I'm a rare gem."

Dro laughed. "Rare gems go in jewelry. I got a couple nice iced out watches. I'm good."

She laughed. "I like a funny man. Keep it up and I might give you a discount."

After sharing a laugh, Dro asked a question he wanted to know since he met her and Nipsey.

"How do Nipsey do it? How is this crazy white dude pimping? How he get you?"

She smiled like she had heard the question a time or two. "Information."

Dro raised an eyebrow. "What that mean?"

"I shouldn't be telling you this, but I kinda like you. Basically he knows people and he doesn't let the girls get close to the trick. Everything goes through me because he trusts me the most. The men can't contact the girls. If they do and he finds out, he cuts them off. And the money is so good that the girls stay true."

Dro nodded. Footsteps in the hall made him swallow his follow up comment. Nipsey walked in the room mumbling.

"Cunt-ass fuck in the booty bitch tryna play me. How a bitch gon' tryna play a P, Dro? Huh, mane? I do er'thang for my bitches. Nivea, cancel Crystal's bitch hoe slut cum bucket bitch ass. I'm tired of her shit."

"Okay, baby. What about Rex?"

He flopped down on the couch and reached for the plate of coke. "I don't know what to do with that snake rat muthafucka yet. I'ma let you know. Now leave me and Young Dro so we can talk." After snorting a big-ass line of cocaine, he turned to his guest. "What's up, young'un? What brings you to the honeycomb hideout?" Sniff. Sniff.

"I'm in a jam and I need some money to pay my lawyer bills."

"You askin for a loan?" Nipsey asked, preparing another line.

"Nah. You know what me and my niggas do. I was hoping you could put me onto somebody with some money. Let me hit 'em."

Nipsey dropped the credit card he was using to separate the dope. He eyed Dro. Then he began the high-pitched laugh. "Oh, hell yeah! Have you ever heard of the book *48 Laws of Power*?"

Dro rolled his eyes. "C'mon, Nipsey. We not about to get into another crazy-ass story, is we?"

The white man looked hurt. "Ouch, man! Pimps got feelings, too."

"I didn't mean it like that. I mean, I did, but I wasn't tryna shit on you."

He smiled. "Good. 'Cause I want to tell you about the famous courtier."

"What the fuck is a courtier?"

"A muthafucka who got favor with royal muthafuckas and shit. Be going to court for 'em and running messages for 'em. In *48 Laws of Power*, it tells that you want your courtier to be proceeded by a good reputation wherever he go. People believe in what everybody else believe. And a man's worth can be caught up in it. You know what I'm sayin'?"

Confusion spread across Dro's face. "Man, what the fuck is you talking about?"

"I want you to be my courtier."

Dro looked even more confused. "Speak plain, man. What is you saying?"

"I want you to be my courtier of death. I want to have my own hitman."

"Is that gon' get me some money to pay my lawyer bills? I'm tryna hit a lick before I leave town, and I'm leavin' as soon as I get Coupe and Dirty."

Nipsey took his time making another line of dope and snorting it. "Okay. I see you, mane." Sniff. Sniff. "I'ma put you on to this sucka muthafucka Rex. This bitch keep tryna dig in my pockets and I don't want him breathing after the night is over. I got a condo in the same building as his. Listen to what I tell you, because I'ma only say it once."

***

Rex Mason was a boss, not because he signed people's paychecks, but because he lived his life the way he wanted. He was loud when he wanted to be. Obnoxious when he wanted to be. He showed off just because he could. And he didn't give a damn what anyone thought about it. At fifty-three years old, he was in good health, but bad shape. Male pattern baldness took most of his hair and what was left was graying and thin. He was short with a pot belly. He had a long nose that looked more like a bird's beak. And he had beady eyes that seemed to always be scheming. But when you were sitting on a net worth of twenty-five million dollars, there was no such thing as ugly. He owned five wineries, twenty rental properties, two trucking companies, and was a minority owner in the Milwaukee Buck's with a five percent stake. Money wasn't a problem. Comfort wasn't a problem. And women weren't a problem. The only problem he had was not being able to find his Viagra pills.

"Dammit! I know I had it in here somewhere," Rex fussed as he searched the drawer next to his bed.

"Hurry up, big daddy," Crystal purred, fingering her swollen clitoris.

Crystal was a fine twenty-eight-year-old brunette with legs that seemed to go on for days, big DD breasts, and a flat booty.

"Wait. Let me check in the master bath. I think we had them in the Jacuzzi last night," he said before going in the bathroom.

"Hurry up, baby! I need you inside me right now. I'm so hot for you."

Crystal continued to play with her pussy while she waited for Rex to find his pills. A noise on the balcony made her pause.

"Rex, is that you out there?"

"I'm in the bathroom. I found them!" he shouted, coming out wearing a big smile. After grabbing the bottle of wine from the table, he popped a pill and washed it down with a drink.

"I heard something on the balcony."

He blew her off and jumped in bed. "It was probably the wind or a bird, baby. We're on the fifth floor."

"Don't you want to take a look just in case? Or at least close the door before the bird flies in here."

Rex reluctantly got out of bed and moved to close the sliding glass door. A tall figure in black appeared from behind the curtain, slapping Rex in the face with a gun.

"Unh!" the old man grunted as he fell to the floor.

Dro and Twenty rushed into the room. They were strapped with pistols, dressed in black, wearing masks and gloves.

"Aaaahhhh!" Crystal screamed, covering her naked body with the Egyptian sheets.

"Shut the fuck up, bitch!" Twenty yelled, pointing the pistol in her face.

"Who are you? What do you want?" Rex groaned, holding his bleeding face.

"We want that safe, bitch. Where it at?" Dro said. He was standing over the old man, pointing the pistol in his face.

"You don't need guns for this. You can have the money. Just get the fuck outta my house," Rex fussed as he struggled to stand.

Dro grabbed his arm to help. "Well, take me to the safe then."

The white man mugged Twenty as they walked towards the door. "Don't you touch her. You hear me? Don't touch my girl!" he warned.

"You mean like this?" Twenty laughed, caressing her face with the gun. "Go get that money before we smoke yo' old ass."

After one last mug, Rex led Dro to the safe in his office. Inside was $275,000.

"There you go. Take it all and get the hell out of my house. How the hell did you get on my balcony anyway? You guys have wings?"

Dro studied the old man for a moment, wondering if he should confess. "It turns out you made an enemy of my friend. Let this be a lesson. Never try to get over on a pimp. Nipsey sends his regards," Dro said before shooting him in the face.

Another pop sounded in the bedroom as Twenty took care of Crystal.

CHAPTER 11

"What's the word on who killed Levi?" Trill asked. He was sitting behind the desk at Flex-n-Shine. Coupe sat on the couch across from him smoking a blunt.

"I don't know yet. I think it might be the same niggas that killed the studio manager. She showed me the video and them niggas wore masks."

"They shot her in the face and didn't rob her. It seems personal," Dirty spoke up.

Trill looked in the shooter's direction. "Keep talkin'. Tell me who you think did it? What about the niggas that robbed Bam-Bam?"

Dirty shook his head. "Nah. Them Bender niggas ain't no killas. They just wanted the money. I'ma pay them niggas a visit soon. But real shit, I think it might be them Savage niggas. Dro still out there. I tried to murk him, but missed. Got his bitch. He got Levi's brother, Zero. Niggas is killas and they be bringing heat when they come."

Coupe nodded. "I forgot about that bitch-ass nigga. Now that you said it, I think it's him, too. That fuck nigga gettin' on my nerves."

Trill listened to the explanation. "Why them niggas ain't dead yet? I put a hunnit G's on they heads. They shoulda been in pine boxes. What the fuck?"

"Dirty tried. Put Twenty in the hospital. He locked up right now for killin' Cherry and Keese."

"Puttin' a nigga in the hospital ain't good enough. These niggas need to die. They steady killin' our niggas and we ain't doin' shit."

"They name Savage for a reason." Dirty said. "They ain't no rudy poo-ass niggas. They valid. And they fuck shit up. No disrespect, Coupe, but you see how they did Monster and his shooters. Came in his house and killed the nigga's family. They really 'bout that action. But I want that hunnit G's so I'ma keep my eyes and ears open."

Trill looked back and forth between Dirty and Coupe. "A'ight. I guess we can't do nothin' but stay on point. What the streets sayin' about the twenty percent increase?"

Coupe chuckled. "They don't like it. But we got the best shit in the city so they gon' still shop. I think we still doing the same numbers. I'ma 'bout to go check the traps when I leave here. I'ma get you some numbers later."

After leaving the auto detail shop, Coupe and Dirty hopped in the Benz truck. They roamed the city, checking trap houses.

"Why you didn't take Monster's spot as a partner? Why you let Trill take all the shine?" Dirty asked from the passenger seat.

"Real shit, I didn't want that responsibility. It takes a lot of time and patience to run all this shit. I didn't want the headache."

"So you always wanna be a worker?"

Dirty's words stung a little. Coupe got aggressive. "I ain't no worker, nigga. I'm a boss."

Dirty laughed. "You don't gotta flex up on me, my nigga. I'm just callin' it how I see it. Trill is the top dawg. He calls the shots. He's the boss. You might be a boss in yo' own mind, but make no mistake about it, Trill is that nigga. He the one that make the moves. He the one that upped them prices. You work for him."

Coupe was quiet, thinking. "I never thought about it like that. Trill's like a big brother to me. I always thought him and Monster was gon' be partners. And once bro got killed, I didn't even think about tryna step up to that level. But now that I'm thinkin' about it, I feel like I shoulda did something. You think I should holla at him about it?"

"If I was in yo' shoes, I woulda been said something. But if you not ready for the responsibility, stay in yo' lane."

Dirty wanted to smile, but he didn't. He kept his face neutral and smiled on the inside. The seed had been planted. All he had to do was sit back and watch it grow. By the time Coupe parked in front of Bam-Bam's trap, the issue had already been settled. Coupe would ask for a seat at the table.

"This nigga better have my shit," Coupe mugged, climbing from the luxury whip.

"You know he don't." Dirty laughed. "You didn't give him no time to get it."

Bam-Bam answered the door with a pistol in hand. Travis was in the background, also clutching heat.

"I see you niggas on point." Coupe nodded.

"Niggas ain't finna catch us nappin' no more." Bam-Bam said, tucking the pistol and locking the door.

"Good. What them numbers look like? You got my money yet, nigga?"

"Nah. I had to work my way back up. If you woulda fronted me, I coulda been had it."

"What you got?"

Bam-Bam shifted nervously. "Like ten thousand."

Coupe frowned. "That's it? I thought you was a hustla?"

"I am. But I had to start from scratch. Gimme a couple more days and I'ma have it."

"You outta time, nigga. Gimme my shit."

When Bam-Bam pulled out the money, Coupe snatched it.

"You still owe me fifty G's, nigga. And I want my shit. You got a week. If I don't got my shit, you gon' have to holla at Dirty."

Bam-Bam glanced at the silent killer. The Minnesota native exhaled violence. The youngster didn't want that smoke.

"Gimme five back and let me flip it. I told you I can have it in a couple days."

"Nah, nigga. This my money now. Get my shit."

Bam-Bam mugged Coupe, looking like he wanted to do him bodily harm. "Man, why you gotta be on that weak-ass shit all the time? You know I'ma get you the money, nigga. You making it hard by taking that what I got. The more money I got, the more shit I can buy."

Coupe closed the distance between them. "Who you talkin' to like that?"

Bam-Bam was 6'2" and one hundred ninety pounds. Coupe came to his chest. Instead of backing down, the young thug swelled up and put more bass in his voice. "I'm talking to you, nigga. That shit you doing is some emotional-ass sucka shit."

Coupe took a swing, catching Bam-Bam on the jaw. The punch was weak. More like a slap. The bigger man took it like a champ then returned a punch of his own, catching Coupe in the eye.

"Ahhhh, shit!" Coupe screamed, grabbing his face and falling to the floor.

Dirty snatched the big young'un by the shirt. After shoving him into the wall, he snatched the pistol from Bam-Bam's waist and put it to his head. "Fuck wrong with you, boy?"

"That nigga hit me. I ain't finna let no nigga hit me. Y'all told me to fuck a nigga up if he violate me, no matter if my momma or the president there."

Dirty remembered the words spoken by Coupe and released the youngster.

"Fuck that nigga up, Dirty! Get that bitch-ass nigga!" Coupe screamed.

Dirty gave Bam-Bam the pistol back. "Nah. You told him to fuck a nigga up if they violated him. That's what he did. I respect the li'l nigga's gangsta."

Coupe became irate. "Fuck that! You my shooter. That nigga hit me. Put 'm down."

Dirty chuckled, eyeing Bam-Bam. "He good. Matter of fact, I'ma pay that tab. I like the li'l nigga. But you owe me, Bam. I'm takin' yo' debt."

Bam-Bam nodded. "Good looking."

"I need you to ride with me tonight. Get yo' gun dirty. I'ma take you under my wing and show you how to get down on some niggas. I'ma hit you later. Be ready."

***

"Hell yeah, bitch! Gimme this ass!" LB yelled, slapping Marquesha's little brown booty cheeks. He had her doggy style, sticking dick in her ass.

"Yeah, daddy! Slap my ass again. Fuck me harder!" she cried.

LB shook his long dreads like a wild man while he spanked her ass and fucked her. Beads of sweat dripped down his face as he demonstrated on his side bitch. He kept her stashed, coming over when he wanted to fuck. She let him do what he wanted, how he wanted. Today it was all out ass fucking.

Slap! Slap! Slap!

"You like it like that, bitch?"

"Oh, yeah, daddy! Oh yeah!"

When he was about to bust, LB pulled out and began jacking off. "Come get this, baby."

Marquesha spun around and opened wide. He stuck his feces-covered dick in her mouth. She swallowed his dick and seed.

"Aw shit!" LB panted. He fell back onto the bed after she drained him.

Marquesha lay next to him and cuddled. Both were sweating from a couple rounds of hot and sweaty sex. They had been together for six months. Marquesha didn't care that she was the side chick. She knew her role and played it well.

"Damn, nigga! That dick fire. You need to give it to me full time and quit playin'."

"C'mon, shawty. You know how we do. Play yo' part. We good."

She reached up to kiss him. "I know. I'm just on my Jeremih shit. I wish I could fuck you all the time."

A knock on the front door interrupted their moment.

"See who that is," LB said, reaching for a cigarette.

Marquesha threw on a T-shirt and went to get the door. "Who is it?"

"Showtime. LB over here?"

She unlocked the door. On the front porch was a tall, dark-skinned nigga with dreads.

"What's up, nigga?"

Showtime looked her over as he stepped in the apartment. "What up, shawty? I see you just got yours. Where that nigga at?"

"He in the room."

Showtime closed the distance between them, wrapping her in a hug and palming her ass. "Don't act like this ass ain't mine too. You know that nigga can't fuck you like I do."

She blushed, loving the excitement of fucking two niggas. "You know I ain't forgot. Come through later and put it down, baby."

After a sloppy kiss, they broke the embrace. Showtime walked into the bedroom while Marquesha went to the bathroom.

"What up, fool-ass nigga?" LB greeted, extending a hand.

"What's good, my nigga? How you feeling?"

"Like a king." LB smiled, blowing out a nicotine cloud.

"Fa sho'. Get'cho bitch ass up and come make a run wit' me. I gotta go check on Jason's bitch ass. Make sure that nigga gettin' that money and ain't fuckin' off my pack."

"A'ight. Lemme get dressed real quick."

Showtime stepped out of the room to give his nigga some privacy. He went to the bathroom and found Marquesha bending over the tub. She was running a bath, T-shirt riding high, showing off her ass.

"Let me hit it like that real quick." He smiled, slapping her bare cheeks.

"Boy, stop!" She laughed, hiking her booty higher in the air. "You gon' get us caught. Get out."

Showtime remained. "Fuck that nigga. You my bitch."

She stood and took off the shirt, showing her naked body. Excitement shone in her eyes as she stepped into the tub. "So, what you gon' do? If LB see us, he gon' be mad. But I don't care. It's on you."

Showtime stared at her naked body lustfully, his dick getting harder by the second. He wanted to join her in that water. But LB was his nigga and he couldn't let a bitch come between them.

"I'ma holla at you later. I'm comin' over and beatin' that pussy up," he said before copping a feel and leaving.

"Where my bitch?" LB asked, walking out of the bedroom and just missing Showtime leaving the bathroom.

"Bitch in the bathroom. I needed to get in and piss."

LB walked to the bathroom and found her in the tub. "I'm 'bout to make a run wit' my nigga. I'ma holla at you later, a'ight?"

"Okay, baby. Get at me when you can."

The dreadlocked duo left the confines of Marquesha's apartment and hopped in the green box Chevy parked out front. Twenty-six inch chrome had the old school sitting high. LB let the pipes purr while he found Young Dro's song, "Fresh".

"Man, I love that li'l bitch," he admitted.

"She's a thotiana, brah. All these Bender hoes be J's."

"I think I'm the only one hittin' that. Her pussy stay tight. If anotha nigga is hittin' it, he got a li'l-ass dick."

Showtime laughed. "Yeah, I hear you. Just don't be surprised when you find out you ain't the only one. And it ain't the nigga's fault. It's that hoe's fault."

LB glanced at his nigga as he put the car in drive. "You actin' like you know something? Who fuckin' my bitch?"

Showtime was about to respond when something caught his eye. Two niggas in black rushed from the side of the building, their arms outstretched, pointing pistols. He reached for the Taurus in his waist.

"Pull off, nigga!"

Instead of listening and driving away, LB looked to see what Showtime was talking about and caught a bullet to the face.

Pop, pop, pop, pop, pop, pop, pop, pop, pop, pop, pop!

Dirty and Bam-Bam rushed the car, letting their heaters go. Both men had thirty round sticks in their pistols. They lit the green Chevy up. They stood outside the car, pumping bullets into the victims. More than twenty bullets filled the bodies. It was overkill.

***

"What you know about wine?" Lana smiled, taking the bottle of vintage Merlot from Dro.

"Not much," he admitted. "When Bianca told me you was a wine drinker, I got the most expensive bottle they had at the liquor store. I figured it was the best if it cost the most."

"That's not always the case, but I like Merlot. I'ma put the bottle in the freezer and let it chill. We can have it with dinner," she said, putting the bottle in the freezer before turning her attention back to the stove.

Dro checked her out while she got busy deep frying the perch. Lana was dressed comfortably in a blue Nike T-shirt, leggings, and flip flops. Her body had him gone in the head. Her ass was super fat. It was perfectly round, like God took his time sculpting those cheeks. Thick thighs. Small waist. And she was fine. Bright eyes. Juicy lips. A nice smile. Blonde hair pulled into a pony tail.

"You need some help?" he offered.

She looked over her shoulder. "Can you cook?"

"The basics. Macaroni. A sandwich. A bangin'-ass Ramen noodle," he joked.

"I need a little more than a sandwich and a soup." She laughed. "How about you make us a salad then? I got some fresh lettuce and tomatoes in there. Some shredded cheese and ranch dressing."

He opened the fridge and looked around. "You got some eggs?"

"Yeah. In the side compartment. You know how to boil eggs, right? I know it ain't as fancy as Top Ramen," she cracked.

"Ay, you need to appreciate this experience. How many niggas you know gon' help you in the kitchen the first time they come to yo' house?"

"You got a point there. Some niggas be straight up scrubs and losers. But you cool, Ruben. I'm just giving you a hard time. At least you can hold a decent conversation."

"Decent conversation?" He frowned. "Woman, I debated with scholars while you was riding around in yo' ambulance overcharging people for rides to the hospital. I'm certified."

"Yeah right!" She laughed. "You ain't debated nobody but the weed man about the price. And for your information, I save lives. I'm a paramedic. First responders save more lives than doctors. Get it right. I'm Superwoman."

Dro nodded. "I'll give you that, since you do save people. But don't mistake my street side for lack of knowledge. I'm more than what you see."

She turned to face him, a challenge in her eyes. But she didn't get to issue it because Alana walked in the kitchen.

"Mama, something wrong with my tablet," the four-year-old whined.

"Let me see it. What did you do?"

"Nothing. I was watching YouTube videos and then it went out."

Dro stood and watched the mother and daughter interact. They looked just alike. Thoughts of Asia jumped into his head, a longing for his baby grabbing at his soul.

"There you go, baby," she said after restarting the device.

"Thanks, Mommy. When the food gon' be ready? I'm hungry."

"In a minute, baby. Go watch the videos. I'll call you when it's ready."

Dro watched the little girl bounce happily from the kitchen. He remembered when his daughter was her age. The hole in his heart grew bigger by the moment.

"You okay?" Lana asked, looking over and seeing the pained look on his face.

He snapped out of the zone, blinking away tears that threatened to spill. "Yeah. I was just thinking about somebody," he said, turning away and putting the eggs in a pot of boiling water.

Lana got curious. "You got kids?"

"I had a daughter," he mumbled.

Lana looked heartbroken. "Had? What happened?"

He could feel the tears fighting to be released and kept his back turned so she wouldn't see the pain. "She got killed."

"Oh my God! What happened?"

"State Fair shooting a couple months ago."

Her eyes popped. "That was you?"

"Yeah. Me and some of the family."

"Damn, man. I'm sorry to hear that," she said, reaching out to rub his arm.

"Yep. Hey, let's talk about something else. That's not a good subject for me."

"Yeah. Sure. Um, how do you like your fish?"

"Like all black people. With a lot of hot sauce."

After dinner was over, Lana bathed the toddler and put her to bed. Then the grownups retired to the living room to drink wine and kick it. Dro noticed the Bible on the end table opened to the book of Hebrews.

"You read the Bible every day?"

"No. I try to, but sometimes I forget. I like the daily devotionals. What about you?"

"Nah, I don't read it. I used to. I would rather listen to good preaching. No matter how deep in the streets I am, I always felt attached to God. Like he was watching over me. I had some situations that I shouldn't have made it out of. Life or death shit. Dude really be looking out for me."

She looked impressed. "Wow. I like hearing that and agree. That's deep. You was raised in church, huh? You a PK?"

He laughed. "Hell nah, I ain't no preacher's kid. But we was raised in church."

Lana rested manicured feet on Dro's lap. "You got brothers or sisters?"

"Yeah. Two little sisters. Kailah and Shanice. They my heart," he said, massaging her feet.

Lana gushed. "Aw. That is so cute. I'm the oldest of three too. You met Bianca. I have a little brother, Brian. He swears he's hard and wanna be called Bam-Bam. But he soft. Tryna be a drug dealer, but don't know the first thing about the streets."

Dro watched her talk, but wasn't paying much attention to the words. He loved watching her lips. They were juicy and moist from the wine. He wanted to kiss them. She noticed the look he was giving.

"Why you lookin' at me like that, man?"

"Can I be real with you, Lana?"

She recognized the look of hunger in his eyes. "Yeah. What's on your mind?"

"I'm really feeling you. Everything about you. You spiritual. You funny. Smart. I even like that you save people. I think it's noble. And yo' lips is doing something to me right now. Got me wanting to know what it would be like to kiss you. You seem like you would fully give yo'self in a kiss, too. Like it would be thoughtful and tender."

106

A chill went through her body as a lustful fire lighting in her eyes. "Whoo, Ruben! I'ma need you to slow down," she said, sitting up and pulling her feet from his lap.

"My bad. I didn't mean to make you uncomfortable."

"You not making me uncomfortable. You making me hot," she said, fanning herself with her hand.

"My bad. I'm just really into you and I wanna get to know you. I ain't tryna be disrespectful, but I wanna fuck you. Seem like you might be a little nervous at first. But I bet when you relax and get in the moment, we can get lost in the zone. I know it would be good."

Lana set the glass of wine on the table and ran a hand through her hair. Her legs were shaking, her breathing rapid. Then she lunged at Dro, sucking his lips in her mouth, attacking his face. The kiss was deep and passionate. Her lips felt like moist pillows. They moved around on the couch like wrestlers, ripping at each other's clothes. When they were naked, she fondled his tool while he paused to check out her body. Shorty was banging. Big hard nipples. Dark areolas. Flat stomach. Slim waist. Wide hips. A fat shaved pussy. Before he could decide how to take her, she pulled him between her legs, guiding his dick into her pussy.

"Ahh, yeah!" she moaned.

"Oh shit!" Dro grunted, pushing into her until they were pelvis to pelvis.

If there was a prize for having the best pussy, he would have given it to her three times. After her walls adjusted to him being inside, Dro got busy, giving her the D. He short stroked, long stroked, hit it hard, and hit it soft. Lana expressed her pleasure with moans of ecstasy and nails digging into the skin of his back. When he felt himself about to bust, he stopped.

"Bend over the couch," he told her, wanting to get it from the back.

Lana bent over the armrest, slapping her big booty. "Hit it good, baby."

Dro admired the flesh of her backside before diving deep inside. He hit it hard, loving the way her ass rippled and bounced against his pelvis and stomach. When he busted his first nut, he knew they probably wouldn't be getting any sleep that night.

CHAPTER 12

"I think it's time for me to go, my nigga."

Twenty turned his head slowly, faded from the Crown Royal and blunt of strong. "Why you say that, my nigga?"

Dro let out a long breath, taking his time to think of the right words. They were sitting in Twenty's living room, getting fucked up and watching *Boyz in the Hood*. The movie made Dro reflect on his life. He had been through so much. The word from the family preacher confirmed what he felt in his heart. It was time to go.

"When I went to church with the fam, the preacher talked about listening to the still small voice. Going when it tells you to go. Doing what it tells you to do. My nigga, my whole life the voice inside been guiding me. And when I didn't listen, I got fucked up. I'm in so much shit. America's body. Monster. 'Bout to be fucked with this Shamika shit. I feel it in my gut, my nigga. God telling me it's time for me to go."

Twenty was silent for a moment. Dro thought he nodded off.

"You know what, brah? I never really understood the whole God talking to me shit. I feel certain shit in my gut and I can hear myself talking in my head. But all the years I been alive, I never heard the voice of God. I went to church. Moms told me about Jesus and to pray. But every time I try to pray, I don't feel shit. It feels like I'm talking to me. So a long time ago I came to the conclusion that I'ma be my own god. Not the invisible super powerful muthafucka up in heaven. I ain't sure if that's real. But I'm my own god because I make my own decisions and follow my instincts. I listen to the voice inside my head. That's how I made it all this time, my nigga. I trust myself more than I could trust in anything. I know I won't let myself down, you know?"

Dro took a long drag on the blunt before passing it to Twenty. "I hear you, my nigga. That shit make all the sense in the world. I just feel like it's something bigger than us out there. Something had to create all this shit. I don't believe we just happened. And I put my faith in whatever created me. Us. This planet. It's gotta be more to life than this. It's gotta be. This can't be it."

"What if it is? What if all we get is this one shot to live? No heaven. No hell."

Dro was silent. Thinking. "Shit, I don't know."

"That's what I'm sayin, my nigga. Don't nobody know."

The Savages became silent, getting lost in thought and the movie.

"What about Dirty and Coupe? I thought you wanted to get them niggas."

"I guess it wasn't meant to be. I gotta get the fuck outta here before I don't get the chance to leave. Fuck them niggas. They can have this shit. I'm tryna stay free."

***

Detective Jackson had been a good guy once. And as he sat in the cruiser, staring out at the night, he knew that those days were long gone. At forty-three years old, life had tossed him around like a sailboat boat on the ocean in a perfect storm. He had married and divorced. Twice. Lost his wife, family, and friends to the job. Being a good cop meant that you were bad at everything else. Chasing leads was more important than being a good husband. Catching criminals was more exciting than watching his son play football. And now he was alone. At first he hated it. But after five years of coming home to an empty house, he got used to it. Plus, he was a good detective. He solved homicides like nobody's business. And he was so caught up reflecting that he didn't see the man creeping towards the car with his gun drawn.

"Hey! Gimme your money!"

Jackson flinched, scared as hell. Detective Scott busted out laughing.

"Why the fuck you play so much, Mark!" Jackson snapped, wanting to get out of the car and beat his ass.

"Yo' scary ass!" Scott continued laughing. "Froze up like a bitch. Soft-ass nigga."

"I'ma show yo' ass soft. Keep talkin' shit and I'ma put yo' li'l punk ass in the trunk again. Get in the car, nigga."

Scott continued laughing as he climbed in the passenger seat. "Only reason you got me the first time was 'cause you crept up on me when I wasn't looking. Try that shit again and I'ma put yo' big ass down."

"You ain't gonna do shit. Did you take care of what you needed to take care of in there?"

Scott adjusted the crotch of his pants. "Yeah. Bitch didn't even know how to suck dick right. But she had some good pussy. How a bitch that get paid to fuck don't know how to give head? You shoulda came in and ran a train on her with me. Her booty was so big that I damn near wanted to fuck her in the ass, but I ain't with that homo shit."

"Anal sex ain't homo shit, nigga. You just got a li'l dick and that big ass had you intimidated."

"Fuck you, nigga. You just with that gay-ass shit. Asses wasn't made for dicks. Pussy is though. If yo' ass go to prison, you gon' fit right in."

"You'll be going before I do, fucking with them prostitutes. Hope you didn't leave no DNA."

Scott thought for a moment. He remembered the used condom in the garbage. "Bitch bet' not say nothing or I'ma get her ass on all kinds of charges. I'll make up some shit. And you gon' back me up."

Jackson nodded. "Again. You goin' in before I do."

"Fuck you, nigga. Drive down on Zoe's bitch ass so I can get a couple dollars before I call it a night."

The unmarked sedan cruised through the Milwaukee night, the detectives lurking. They watched the street like hitmen trying to catch a mark. Twenty minutes later, Jackson parked outside a gray ranch style house on the west side. The men left the car and walked upon the porch cautiously. Jackson knocked on the door loudly.

"Who is it?" a female called from inside.

"The police! Open the door!" Scott yelled.

Locks clicked. When the door opened, a young pregnant white woman stood in the doorway. "Zoe's not here."

Scott pushed past her. "Move out the way. Zoe? I know you in here. Yo' car outside, dumb ass. Where you at?"

"Y'all can't come in without a warrant. This is against the law!" the woman argued.

"Shut up and sit down, Amber," Jackson said, pushing the woman onto the couch while they looked around.

It only took a couple minutes to find their man. He was hiding under a pile of dirty clothes in a bedroom closet.

"Get'cho ass up outta here!" Scott said, snatching the man up by the back of his shirt.

Zoe was a short, husky man in his late thirties. He had dark skin, thinning hair, and wore a pair of jean shorts with no shirt. "C'mon, man! What you doing, Scott? I didn't do nothing."

"I didn't say you did shit. Come out here and sit down. We need to talk."

Scott led Zoe to the living room. He pushed him down on the couch next to his baby mama.

"Don't be pushing him like that!" the woman yelled, cradling her man in her arms. "You okay, baby?"

"How is it your sixteen-year-old girlfriend got more heart than you?" Scott laughed, looking at Zoe like he was a sucka.

"C'mon, man. What the fuck y'all want? Y'all can't be just popping up like this," Zoe whined.

"I'm seventeen," Amber corrected. "My birthday was three days ago."

Scott waved her off. "Stay in a kid's place. Zoe, I need some money. What you got for me?"

He looked like he wanted to cry. "C'mon, Scott. I just gave you three thousand last week."

"And I spent it. Gimme a grand."

"We don't got no more money." Amber mugged him.

Scott pulled out his cuffs. "Well, then I gotta take yo' man in. Y'all know how this goes by now. Get up, Zoe. Put yo' hands behind yo' back. You being arrested for statutory rape. Jackson, search the house. I know he got some boy and a pistol in here."

Jackson made a move towards the back of the house.

"Wait!" Zoe yelled. "Okay. All I got is five hundred."

Scott smiled. "I need that G."

"C'mon, man. You taking all my fuckin' money and I'm 'bout to have a shorty. Show some compassion, nigga."

"A'ight. Gimme seven hunnit and some info."

Zoe nodded to his girl. "Go get him the money, baby."

Scott watched the white girl walk to the back of the house. "She got a nice ass. You teach her how to suck dick?"

Zoe mugged him. "Stay away from my girl. This between me and you."

"She's too young for me, my nigga. I just wanted to know if she could suck dick. I heard white girls like to give head."

Zoe looked to Jackson. "Get yo' boy, man."

Jackson laughed. "I think he got jungle fever. And a thing for fuckin' girls in the ass. Keep her in the house."

Scott mugged his partner. "Fuck you, nigga. A'ight, Zoe. Tell me what you know about the Savages. You heard anything about Dro?"

Zoe rolled his eyes and let out a breath. "C'mon, man. You know I don't know them niggas. I ain't with that jack boy shit."

"I'm just checking. If you hear something, make sure you let me know. That'll go a long way to showing me that you on my side."

"A'ight. If I hear somethin, I'ma call."

After getting the money from Amber, the detectives were on their way. It was ten minutes past eleven o'clock and the men were about to call it a night.

"You need to use some of that money to get your car fixed," Jackson said as he pulled up outside Scott's house.

"Why I need a car when I got you? All this is going to Kasha. I gotta pay her a visit tomorrow night." Scott laughed as he opened the door. "I love you, baby. Make sure you be here to get me at eight on the dot."

"Fuck you and I hate you." Jackson laughed. "Now get the fuck out."

The coppers were caught up in their banter and didn't see the two figures dressed in black. They emerged from the side of Scott's house. In Dro's hand was a 12 gauge Mossberg pump with an infra-red beam. Twenty held an AK-47. Scott was getting out of the car when he noticed the red dot on his chest. Dro smiled as he pulled the trigger.

Kaboom! The shotgun erupted, fire shooting out of the barrel like it was a dragon. The slug hit the cop in the chest, lifting him off his feet and slamming him into the car.

Brrrrreaaaaatttt! Brrrrreaaaaatttt! The AK-47 spat, lighting up the night. High-powered rounds tore into the police car's frame. Jackson tried to drive away, but the chopper bullets punctured his body, making him lose control of the vehicle. He crashed into a parked car. Dro ejected the empty shell and chambered another round as he ran up on Scott. Milwaukee's finest lay on the curb shaking uncontrollably as the goon stood over him. Dro looked him in the eyes as he put the gauge to his face. Kaboom!

While Dro finished his kill, Twenty ran towards the wrecked cruiser, letting off shots. When he got to the car, Jackson was slumped over the steering wheel. Just to make sure he wouldn't live, Twenty stood outside and filled Jackson's body with bullets.

***

The bus ride to Twin Forks, North Dakota took ten hours. Dro didn't sleep during the trip. His thoughts were jumbled. So much blood covered his hands that it was hard to see anything good left in his soul. His body felt polluted. All the work he put in in the streets had finally become too much. The body count was high. He began to wonder if forgiveness of sins was real. Would God really look past everything he'd done? He also thought about what he was going to say to Forever. They hadn't spoken in two weeks. It felt like a lifetime had passed since they'd been in each other's presence. He wasn't sure how to say everything that needed to be said. And he remained at a loss for words when the bus pulled into the terminal. A ten minute Uber ride took him to the front of Spencer's house. After grabbing the Gucci bag and paying the driver, he walked on the porch and rang the doorbell.

"Who is it?"

When he heard Forever's voice, an indescribable warmth entered his chest.

"Ruben."

When the door opened, Forever launched herself into his arms. "Oh my God! I can't believe it's you!" she cried.

Dro held on tightly, rubbing her ass and loving the feel of his girl back in his arms. "I told you I was gon' come."

She pulled back enough to give him the best "I miss you kiss" that he'd ever had. Then they just stared at each other. Dro couldn't get past how fine his girl was. Nivea who? The expensive prostitute didn't have nothing on his baby momma. Her dark curly hair shined. Flawless light brown skin glowed. Tears stained her slanted brown eyes. Full lips and a perfect smile completed the prefect face. She was seven months pregnant and her stomach had gotten bigger.

"I missed you so much!" She grinned.

"I missed you, too. Now let me in."

"Sorry. Come in. Why didn't you tell me you were coming?" she asked, locking the door.

"Because I wanted to see the look you got right now. How is my li'l man?" he asked, putting a hand in her stomach.

"He's fine. Healthy. How are you doing? Did you figure out your legal situation? Are the police still looking for you?"

He nodded, letting out a stressed breath. "Yeah, baby. And if they catch me, they gon' cook me. I'm running."

Tears filled her eyes. "How bad is it? Did you kill somebody?"

He didn't lie. "Yeah."

Her eyes grew wide. "No, Ruben! Why? What happened?"

"It don't matter what happened. They dead. I did what I had to do. You might see it on the news, but don't believe everything they say. You know me. Everything that I did was for survival. To get back to you and our son. I love y'all more than anything I've ever loved in my whole life and I would do anything for y'all. This is to help you." He gave her the Gucci bag.

Forever frowned. "What is this?"

"Some money. Sixty thousand. That's everything I got. Take it so you and li'l Ruben can have a good start. Use it to put a down payment on a house. I'ma send some more when I can."

"Wait. You're not staying?"

"I can't." He shook his head, getting choked up. "I gotta go where don't nobody know me. I'm in some serious shit, baby."

She grabbed hold of his arm. "No. Don't leave me, Ruben. Or take me with you. I don't want to be without you again."

"You can't come with me, Forever. It's too dangerous and you gon' slow me down. I need to be able to move on a dime and I can't do that if I'm worried about you and the baby. I want y'all safe. That's gon' make it easier for me."

Forever wrapped him in a hug and cried. "I don't want you to go, baby. I don't want to do this on my own. I want Junior to have a father."

"I know, baby. But we gotta deal with what we got. I'ma come back. I just need some time to get myself situated. I came back this time. Trust that I'm comin' back again."

Forever broke the embrace and they began staring at each other again. Like they were trying to remember each other's faces.

"I'm going to wait for you. You better bring your ass back to me, Ruben. I swear to God, you better come back."

"Did you just cuss?" He laughed.

Her face remained serious. "That's how much I mean my words. Bring your ass back home."

"I'm coming back, baby, I promise."

"You better. Now come to my room and make love to me. I don't know the next time I'll see you, so make it good. My dad doesn't come home for three more hours."

CHAPTER 13

Leaving Forever was one of the hardest things Dro had ever done. During the bus ride to Atlanta, all he could think about were the tears. She cried like it was his funeral. Seeing her pain was torture. He thought about staying just so she would stop crying, but he had to go. It was best for everybody. And the sight of her sad face would be etched into his head and become the motivation to survive and get back to her and li'l Ruben.

The bus didn't reach Atlanta until the next day. He breathed a sigh of relief when it pulled into the terminal. No one knew him here. It was time for a new start.

"Excuse me." He tapped the woman sitting next to him. "My phone died. Can I use yours to call my ride?"

"Yeah. Sure."

After dialing Whisper, he waited.

"Yeah?"

"Whisper, this Dro. I'm at the bus station. Send me a ride."

"Okay, baby boy. I'm 'bout to send one of my girls. You remember Prianka, right?"

"Yeah."

"Look for a white Benz. Welcome to the A, my nigga."

Thirty minutes, later a cocaine-white E class Benz pulled into the lot. An Indian woman sat behind the steering wheel with Prada glasses atop her head.

"Hi, Dro!" She smiled, looking like a movie star.

"What up, Prianka? I see Atlanta treating you good." He smiled, climbing in the passenger seat.

"I love it here. It's always lit. How long you here?"

"Probably for the long haul. I burnt up the Mil."

She smiled, knowing not to ask any more questions. "Well, this is a good place to be if you want a new start. I hope everything works better for you here."

The Hoe Whisperer's new crib was a one point five million dollar mansion in the Decatur. The glossy black paint had gold flecks, making the baller pad shine from the outside. On the inside was seven bedrooms, five bathrooms, a rec room, an indoor pool and sauna, and a five car garage.

"Damn!" Dro whistled, eyeing the phat crib as he stepped from the Benz. "Whisper stepped his shit all the way up."

The inside of the house was just as nice as the outside. Twenty foot ceilings. Marble floors. Big-ass winding stair case. Whisper stood on the top step dressed in a tailored lime green suit, a white bucket hat, and white Gators. His goatee was lined perfectly and his dark skin was shining, reflecting that money was the best lotion.

"What it do, young Dro? Welcome to the Black House. I'm the muthafuckin president!"

"What's good, pimpin? I see you upgraded that loft to something real special."

"That's how bosses do it. Come on up here and chop it up with yo boy. What kinda jam you done got yo'self in?"

Dro climbed the staircase and followed Whisper to a plush great room. Hardwood floors, seventy-inch flat screen, and black Italian leather couches as big as twin-sized mattresses. On the black glass table was a half-pound of loud and all kinds of smoking paraphernalia.

"Chill. Roll you something. Tell me what happened."

Dro grabbed a weed pipe and stuffed it. "Man, Whisper. I set that bitch on fire. The bodies started piling up. I had to stank my baby mama and they got Crush for that because his DNA was on the envelope."

"You killed America?" Whisper asked, surprise lighting his eyes.

"Bitch called me from the county jail tryna set me up 'cause I wouldn't bail her out. Got to askin' me about Monster. So I had Crush leave her mama the money. Then I popped her later that night."

"Damn. That whole situation is fucked up. Especially Crush. He just started gettin' his shit together."

"I know. But that ain't the worst. The nigga Dirty came to my bitch's house right after we finished having a threesome. Killed my bitch, but I got his nigga. I tried to get my bitch's friend to take the case. She was gon' get self-defense. Offered the bitch ten G's, but she wouldn't do it. So I knocked her off. DNA in both of them."

Whisper winced. "Damn. That'll do it right there."

"Yeah, I know. But before I left, me and Twenty killed the police that was investigating us. Jackson and Scott. Hopefully, the investigation gets pushed back. Like I said, I set that bitch on fire."

"You did that." Whisper nodded. "Well, you gon' have to lay low here. Don't be on all that wild shit. We gettin' money. If you be good to the game, the game will be good to you. Ya boy Lunatic turned out to be a natural with this pimp shit. He is doin' big shit."

Dro smiled. "Straight up? Where he at?"

"Out with his girls. He should be back soon. You can stay here as long as you need. So, how you wanna get money? That jack shit is over, right?"

Dro took a hit of the bowl. "Man, I don't know what the fuck I'ma do. I just gave Forever my last sixty for her and the baby."

Whisper eyed him, thinking. "Okay. I'ma put you on as our security until you figure out what you wanna do. If you want, I can show you the ropes in this pimp shit."

Dro chuckled. "Shit, I might have to consider it. But I'ma just lay back for now. Try to stay out of sight."

Whisper stood. "Okay. Sounds good to me. Whatever you wanna do. I gotta make a couple moves and check on some shit. The house is yours. Lunatic should be back. We got a party at Liv tonight."

Dro got high and checked out the mansion before settling down to watch semi-pro basketball on the seventy-inch TV. An hour later, he heard movement downstairs. He walked to the end of the hall and looked over the balcony. Lunatic walked in with three bad bitches. When he saw Dro upstairs, the men had a stare down. The new school pimp didn't look happy to see his day one.

"What you doin' here?"

"Damn. Love really is lost, huh?"

"Who is that?" one of the women asked.

"Don't worry 'bout it. Go find something to do," Luna admonished before turning back to Dro. "What you want me to say, my nigga? That I'm happy to see you? I ain't."

Dro descended the stairs. "You gon' have to get off this fuck shit. I told you what happened. That shit over. Tae gone, brah. Being mad at me ain't gon' bring him back."

Lunatic got mad. "You the one on some fuck shit. You started all that shit. You shoulda killed the girls instead of lying about it. You knew he was gon' be mad once he found out. Then you upped on him in Chicago and put yo' hands in him at the condo. What you think that nigga was gon' do?"

"I didn't think he was gon' try to kill me, nigga. And what you sayin' don't justify that shit. We had a fight. If we was really niggas, he wouldn't have came to my house and tried to kill me. Nigga killed my daughter's dog. He crossed that line first."

Lunatic waved him off, attempting to walk away. "Whatever, nigga."

Dro grabbed his shirt. "Don't blow me off like that, my nigga. Let's talk."

"We ain't got shit to talk about." Lunatic mugged. "Let go of my Versace. This cost too much for you to be gettin wrinkles in it."

Dro got mad and tugged at the shirt. The fabric ripped. "Fuck this shirt, nigga. I'm tryna holla at you, but you on this bullshit."

Lunatic looked down at the tear in his shirt sleeve, then back at Dro. "Bitch-ass nigga!" he cursed, taking a swing.

Dro knew the punch was coming, but couldn't react fast enough. He tried to duck, but Lunatic's knuckles tagged him on the jaw, making him stumble. Then he rushed Dro, swinging wild punches, some of them catching him in the head. When Dro caught his balance, he grabbed Lunatic and they began wrestling. Dro kneed him in the nuts and got the advantage. Lunatic reached for his balls and Dro hit him with a three punch combo that sat him on his ass. Lunatic was done fighting. He reached behind him and pulled a Glock from the small of his back.

"That's how we doin' it?" Dro asked, lifting his hands.

120

Lunatic kept the gun pointed at Dro as he checked his bleeding lips. "Fuck you, nigga! Fuck you!"

"So, you gon' shoot me, huh? You talkin' shit about me and Tae, but you hit me and upped on me."

Lunatic didn't speak. Just mugged.

Dro put his hands down and sat on the floor. "Stop pointing that gun at me before it accidentally go off."

Lunatic lowered the pistol and the gun brothers sat in silence.

"I'm fucked up, Luna. This the only place I got to go. I killed America and Crush got locked up for it. They tryna connect me to it too. Dirty got at me and killed Shamika. I had to kill his nigga and Shamika's friend. My DNA in both them hoes. And me and Twenty whacked Jackson and Scott. I'm fucked up, my nigga. I ain't got nowhere to go. Can we end this shit? I want my nigga back."

Lunatic didn't speak. Just kept on mugging. Then slowly, a smile spread across his face. "Yo' square ass got some hands, nigga." He chuckled, touching his swelling lip again.

Dro got up, pulling Lunatic to his feet. "You my nigga, dawg. And I love you," he said as the men shared a strong embrace.

"You know it's love. My bad for actin' like a sucka. Burying Tae fucked me up. But I'm happy you here. We can show these niggas and bitches in the A how Savages get down."

***

Liv was the hottest club in Atlanta. Anybody that was somebody showed up on Show Off Saturday to flex. Every car in the parking lot cost at least a hundred thousand dollars. Every female was dressed in their sexiest ensemble. Every man loaded his pockets with cash, and neck, wrist, and fingers with ice. Ballers balled. Players played. And stunners stunted. Dro sat in the VIP looking at all the rich, famous, and infamous people party. They threw money around like it grew in their backyard. No one seemed to have a care in the world. The only thing that mattered was having a good time.

While looking out over the party, Dro spotted a bad female by the bar. He made his way over and got the bartender's attention.

"Hey! Can I get another bottle of Rosé?"

She went to the cooler and Dro turned to the woman he had come over to see. She looked even better up close. She had shoulder-length dreads dyed pink. She wore a pair of diamond studded Cartier's and had studs in both cheeks. She had dark brown skin, big titties, and a fat ass covered by a skintight strapless yellow dress. White red bottoms made her stand almost as tall as him.

"Hey. My name Dro. What's up with you?"

She looked him over and smiled, showing off a diamond grill on her bottom row. "Where you from?"

"Milwaukee. Is it that obvious that I'm from out of town?"

"Nah. It's not the way you look. It's that you don't know who I am that let me know you not from here."

He raised an eyebrow, paying for the bottle the bartender set on the bar. "So, who is you?"

"I'm Starlet. PJ's girl."

Dro still didn't see the big deal. "Oh. Okay. You think yo' man would mind if you had a friend?"

She gave a flirty smile. "I don't know. But you can ask him if you want."

"Where he at? Is he here?"

She grabbed her drink and pointed. Dro followed her finger. PJ was a big light-skinned nigga with an uncombed Philly fro. He wore jewelry like a rapper, earlobes hanging from the heavy diamonds in his ears. And he was walking towards Dro, mugging.

"He don't look too happy." Dro laughed.

"He's not. I think you should run."

Dro cut his eyes at her. "I don't run from shit. Fear no man but God."

PJ approached, huffing and puffing. "Why you all up on my shawty, nigga?"

Dro remained calm, popping the bottle and taking a drink. "It wasn't like that, brah. I was just making convo while I got me a bottle. Take it easy, big fella."

He got more aggressive. "Nah, nigga. You take it easy, fuck boy! And move around 'fore I smash yo' ass!"

Dro sized him up. PJ stood 6'6" and 280 pounds. A fight with him would probably be suicide. But that didn't bother the Savage. He made a living in the danger zone. But what he didn't want to do was draw attention on his first night in town. Whisper wanted him to lay low.

"I'ma give you this round, big man. But for future references, check the bitch. Not the nigga," Dro said, walking away.

"Betta watch yo' mouf, pussy-ass fuck nigga!" PJ barked, grabbing his girl's drink and throwing it at Dro's back.

Dro paused when the glass hit him, the cold liquor soaking his shirt. He cocked the bottle of Rosé like a bat, turning and breaking the glass on the big man's face. But the Savage didn't stop there. He let his fists fly, catching PJ with a flurry of punches. The gorilla of a man stumbled backward, falling into the bar. Dro made the mistake of getting too close and got grabbed in a bear hug. PJ tossed him around like a rag doll before security rushed over.

"Ay! Break it up! Break it up!" the bouncers yelled pulling the men apart.

The partygoers all watched as Dro was dragged from the club and thrown on his ass in the parking lot.

"Yo' night over with, brah. Don't come back," D-Bo warned before closing the door.

Dro sat on the ground for a few moments, trying to figure out what the fuck just happened. He had gone from partying, to fighting, to sitting on his ass in the parking lot. Before he could wrap his mind around the events, the door opened again and Whisper stepped out.

"What the fuck don't you understand about staying the fuck out of the way and laying low, li'l nigga?"

Dro stood and dusted himself off. "That wasn't on me, man. That nigga came at me over that bitch and threw a drink on me."

Whisper let out an angry breath. "Dro, that nigga was the last muthafucka you wanted a problem with. That's PJ. Head of Duffle Bag Boyz."

Dro got pissed. "What the fuck I was supposed to do Whisper? Let that nigga treat me like a bitch? You know how we do. Savages ain't no hoes. I didn't start that."

"That ain't the goddamn point, Dro! You supposed to be laying low. We getting money, nigga. We can't be worried about this petty fighting over a bitch shit. You gotta be smarter. You coulda took that and caught the nigga later. Now the whole fuckin' city know. You just whooped the nigga in front of everybody. They gon' be talkin' about this. That nigga gon' wanna hit back."

The door opened again and Lunatic walked out with wide eyes. "Ay, we gon' have to do somethin'. The Duffle Bag Boyz in there mobbin' up."

Dro walked towards the parking lot, looking for the Maserati with his pistol inside. "You strapped, Luna?"

Lunatic ran towards his BMW. "Hell yeah!"

"No! No! No!" Whisper screamed, waving his hands and jumping up and down. "Y'all ain't about to do this shit outside this club. They got cameras and er'body seen what happened inside. Dro, get in the car and take yo' ass home. Let me take care of this."

The club door opened again and ten niggas walked out, looking around. It was the Duffle Bag Boyz.

"Where that nigga at?" PJ yelled, holding a towel on his bloody face.

"Get in the car right now, Dro! Get the fuck in the car!" Whisper yelled.

As much as he wanted to bust the niggas' asses and show them how Savages got down, he respected the OG pimp and climbed in the car.

CHAPTER 14

"Fuck!" Dro cursed, banging the steering wheel as he stopped for a red light. He had only been in Atlanta for a few hours and trouble found him. And from the look in Whisper's eyes, the beef was serious. Damn. He began to wonder if he was cursed with bad luck. Even when he tried to chill, shit still found a way to get at him. He pulled away from the red light, distracted by thoughts of bad luck, when a woman ran into the middle of the street. He smashed the brake, the Maserati sliding to a stop. The woman fell to the ground, unharmed.

"What the fuck you doing?" he snapped, getting out of the car.

She didn't move, staying in the fetal position, her body covered by a wrinkled red dress. And she wasn't wearing shoes.

"Ay, you good?"

She moved slowly, uncurling like a flower. "Why didn't you run me over?" Her accent was heavy, tone aggressive.

"What the fuck is wrong with you? You can't be jumping in front of cars and shit. Get the fuck out the street."

She didn't move. Dro looked around for the police or nosy pedestrians.

"If you don't get yo' ass out the street, I'ma run you over!"

"Do it," she dared, eyes crazy.

He looked around again. "Man, get up. You trippin'. Whatever goin' on in yo' life, it ain't worth dying for."

"Yes, it is. I don't have a reason to live. I want to die."

Headlights in the distance made Dro panic a little. "Listen. I need you to get out the way. I can give you a ride if you want, but I gotta go."

She got up and moved slowly towards the passenger door. "I would like a ride. Please."

He checked her out as they got in the car. She looked Mexican. Brown skin. Long black straight hair. Dark brown eyes. A small nose. Full lips. Healthy teeth. She wasn't beauty queen pretty, but she looked good.

"You gon' have to tell me where to go. This my first time in Atlanta and I don't know my way around."

"I live in Buckhead."

"Where is that?"

"North side. Forty-five minutes from here."

He frowned. "Man, I ain't finna take you all the way over there. I got somewhere to be. You need to find somewhere close."

She didn't appear to be fazed by his change in demeanor. She remained calm.

"I don't have anywhere else. I'm not from here either."

Dro shook his head. The decent part of him wouldn't put her out of the car. "A'ight. I got you. What the fuck you tryna kill yo'self for?"

She hesitated. "I don't want to talk."

"You gon' talk to me. I'm finna give you a forty-five minute ride. My night already fucked up and you made it worse. Why you jumping in front of cars?"

She took her time answering. She kept her head down and mumbled the words. "My boyfriend dumped me."

He glanced over. "You tried to kill yo'self over a nigga?"

She didn't answer.

"I'm Dro. What's yo name?"

"Mariana."

"How old are you?"

"Twenty-two."

"Listen, ma. Ain't no man or woman worth dying over. If they don't want you, move on. You bad. It's way more dogs in the park. You gon' find somebody else. God made somebody for everybody."

They rode in silence for a while.

"Thank you for saying that."

"Yep. Where you from? I hear the accent."

"Mexico."

"How long you been here?"

"Couple months."

"How you get all the way from Mexico to Atlanta?"

"For my boyfriend. My uncle owed and couldn't pay. So he sent me."

Dro's mind connected the dots. Mariana was being trafficked for sex. Instead of selling her, the owner threw her out in the street like garbage. But why? If her uncle owed, why wasn't she sold to a pimp?

"Damn. How you gon get back to Mexico?"

"I'm not going back." She paused. "Will you help me?"

He chuckled. "I don't think I can help you, baby. I'm tryna help myself."

"I have money. And drugs."

That got his attention. "What you say?"

"I can give you money or drugs if you help me."

"Man, stop bullshitting."

"I'm not playing."

He eyed her for a moment. "Where the shit at?"

"At the house. Take me and I give you some."

On the strength that she was Mexican, he believed her. Her owner was probably heavy in the game.

Home turned out to be a mini mansion in the burbs. After parking in the driveway, they walked around to the back door. Mariana began looking around in the bed of granite rocks.

"Fuck you doing?" he asked, getting suspicious.

"Looking for the key. Ah! I found it."

"Whose house is this?"

Something like revenge shown in her eyes. "My boyfriend's. Come in."

He didn't ask any more questions. A blessing had fallen into his lap. He knew an opportunity when he saw one and jumped on it.

"Don't touch nothing that don't need to be touched."

They walked up a flight of stairs and down a short hall into the last room on the left. In the closet were two brown shopping bags. Dro checked the contents. Five bricks of heroin was in one. Two hundred thousand dollars was in the other.

"Is this enough?" she asked.

Dro nodded. "Hell yeah! Let's get the fuck outta here."

From the mini mansion, Dro headed for the Black House. During the ride, he got to know Mariana better.

"Who is the nigga we just took this from?"

"His name is Manny. A drug dealer."

"Who Manny with? He got a squad?"

She nodded. "Hecho en Mexico. In English it means made in Mexico."

Damn. He stole from a Mexican cartel. But he wasn't giving shit back. "Okay. What you wanna do? You got plans."

"My plans were to die. Until I met you. I don't want to go back to being poor in Mexico. I want to stay in America. You can make money, right?"

He rubbed the back of his suddenly aching neck. "Selling dope ain't my thing. Plus, I don't know nobody in Atlanta. And I need to be laying low."

"Everybody in America does drugs. All you have to do is find someone to sell them to."

Her logic was on point. He pulled out the phone and called Whisper. The pimp probably knew a few dealers and users.

"You fucked up this time, Dro," he answered.

"C'mon, Whisper. I told you I didn't start that shit, man. He threw a drink on my back."

"I heard. But Duffel Bag Boyz don't care about that. You from out of town and fucked up they boy. They want war. I'm surprised they let me and Luna leave. They know you came with us. Damn, young'un. I wish you woulda gave him a pass."

"You know I don't draw like that. I'ma gangsta. Ain't no nigga finna disrespect me."

"I know. Where you at?"

"On my way to the Black House. And I got company. I need yo' help with something. It's serious."

"A'ight. We on our way there, too. I'ma holla at you in a minute."

When Dro got to the mansion, Whisper, Lunatic, and a few women were sitting in the great room.

"You fucked that nigga up, brah." Lunatic laughed. "Whole side of the nigga face cut up."

"Do they know where we at?"

"Nah, not yet," Whisper spoke up, checking out Dro's companion. "Who is ya friend?"

"This Mariana. I met her after I left. She part of the reason I need help. We made a move for five thangs of boy. I need to find some buyers."

Lunatic got geeked. "Ooh! My nigga hit a good-ass lick!"

"Who you hit?" Whisper asked.

Dro looked at Mariana. "Nigga name Manny."

"Manny who? Is he plugged?"

"Yeah. She said they named Made in Mexico."

Whisper let out a laugh. "Damn, Dro. You sho' know how to get yo' ass in some shit. Manny is Mexican Cartel. Is that one of his girls?"

He nodded.

Whisper let out a heavy breath. "Dro, you my li'l nigga and my love for you is real. But I think you went too far this time. Cartels ain't no street cliques. They got real money and real connections. This one bad here, mane."

Dro shrugged. "It's too late now. And I ain't givin' it back."

"I know. I'ma make a couple calls and put you in touch with the right people. After I get you connected, you can't stay here no more. You puttin' er'body life in danger. I ain't gon' kick you out on yo' ass but you need to get off the streets fast. Between PJ and the cartel, you gon' need a whole lotta luck to stay out the way."

***

Dro awoke the next morning to a knock on the door.

"Come in."

Mariana poked her head into the room. "Are you awake?"

He sat up in bed. "I am now. What up?"

She came into the room and sat next to him. The wrinkled dress was disheveled from a night of sleep.

"I am hungry. And I need to change clothes. A shower, too."

"It's like five bathrooms in this house. Take a shower. I'ma ask Prianka for some clothes. What kinda food you want?"

"I don't care."

"Order something and have it delivered. I'ma pay for it."

She nodded, staring at him like she wanted to say more.

"What up?"

She smiled. A natural beauty. Woke up looking good.

"Are you bad?"

He chuckled. "What kinda question is that?"

"Yesterday your friends said somebody was trying to kill you. You seem nice, but bad too."

"I don't know how to answer that, Mariana. I'm just me."

"I think everybody has good and bad in them. Nobody is perfect."

He nodded. "I agree."

"Where are you from? How did you get to Atlanta?"

"I'm from up north. Milwaukee, Wisconsin."

"Where is that?"

"All the way at the top of the United States. By Canada."

"That is far. What made you come here?"

"I wanted a new start. Got in some shit. Came here to start over."

"Now you're in more trouble, huh? Because of me?"

"A li'l bit. But you good. I been in trouble way before I met you."

"I think we should leave Atlanta. Go somewhere no one knows us."

"Me too. But first I need to make a connection. So, what's yo' story? Why Manny didn't sell you to somebody to get the money yo' uncle owed? You was bein' trafficked as a sex slave, right?"

She nodded, tears filling her eyes. "Like you, I am good and bad. Manny beat me because I wouldn't do nasty things he wanted. Said I am useless trash and threw me out with garbage."

"Damn. That's fucked up. But it might not been a bad thing that he threw you out, you know? Now we got money. You ever heard the saying, 'one man's trash is another man's treasure?'"

She shook her head and smiled. "No. But I like. Am I your treasure?"

Dro looked towards the bags of money and drugs. "Hell yeah!"

She leaned in and kissed him on the cheek. "Thank you."

He nodded, feeling some type of way about her kissing him. She was a sex slave, and there was no telling what she had done or the diseases she had.

"You're welcome. Order that food and hit the shower. I'ma go find Whisper and see if he got any good news for us."

***

The black Bentley Coupe GT pulled into the park, getting approving looks from those with an appreciation for expensive things. Nore was an Atlanta native. Born and raised on the west side. James P. Brawley Street. By nature, he was a grinder. He started hustling in grade school, bought a bag of suckers for two dollars. There were seventeen inside and he sold them for fifty cents apiece. He learned hustling was all about supply and demand and had been grinding since. Last year, he dropped out of college. He was studying to be an engineer at Morehouse College. After his brother died, Nore gave up on a higher education and tried to imitate his older sibling in the streets. The run was short, but he left the game with a car and a house.

He spotted a white Rolls Royce near the entrance. Whisper and Dro were sitting on a nearby bench.

"Whisperer, what's happening?" He grinned after climbing from the expensive ride.

The pimp gave him daps. "You got it, young fella. This my nephew I was telling you about. Dro."

"What's poppin', mane?"

Dro nodded, sizing Nore up as they shook hands. He had was dark-skinned, average height, with a freshly-cut Boosie fade.

"You got it, my nigga. I like that GT."

Nore nodded. "Yeah, it's a'ight. But that Rolls Whisper got is where it at."

"Wait 'til you see the Rolls truck I'm finna get." The pimp smiled. "I'ma be fucking the city!"

After sharing a laugh, Dro got down to business. "What's up with the hustle, Nore? Whisper told me you plugged into the city. I got some shit I'm tryna get rid of."

Opportunity flashed in the hustler's eyes. "I might know somebody that know somebody. What'chu talkin 'bout?"

"That boy. One hunnit a gram. You put me in with the right people and I'ma straighten you out."

"And it ain't been touched. Straight drop. This a dirt number. You can remix it and won't nobody know," Whisper added.

"Okay. I gotta get in contact wit' a few people. Gimme yo' number."

CHAPTER 15

The Bentley looked out of place in the Target parking lot. Dro sat in the passenger seat feeling a little uncomfortable about the meet. He wanted to be behind the scene to pull Nore's strings like a puppet master.

"How good you know these niggas?"

"They my brother's baby mama's cousins. I been knowing 'em since I was a shorty. Rode bikes and all that shit. While I was in school, they was hustling. They didn't have a big bro tryna push them to do the school shit like I did. Them niggas been out here."

"You know I don't wanna be seen. I'm tryna move this shit and shake this bitch. ATL ain't agreeing with me right now."

"That's why I think you should holla at 'em. They the ones that bought that last batch. It's moving slow because y'all going through me and I neva sold dog food."

Dro considered what he was saying. "A'ight. Soon as Mariana come out, take me to meet these niggas. I'ma see what they talking 'bout."

They didn't have to wait long for the Latin beauty. She came out of the store five minutes later pushing a cart.

"What's all this? I thought you had to get a few items," Dro said, getting out to help her with the bags.

"I did. But if we're going to be living in a hotel, we need some food and clothes and supplies. I want to make it feel a little more comfortable."

He couldn't argue with that. "A'ight. We about to go meet his cousins. They might be able to help us move this shit faster so we can get the fuck outta Atlanta."

K-Man lived twenty minutes from the super store. The sky-blue candy-painted old school Pontiac Lemans on 28s parked out front screamed trap star housing. Dro and Mariana followed Nore up the steps. After ringing the doorbell, they waited.

"Who dat?"

"Nore. Open the door, nigga!"

When it opened, a short dark-skinned nigga with dreads stood in the doorway. "What up, cuz?" He nodded, eyeing Dro and Mariana.

"Let us in. This who I was telling you about. He the plug. Dro, this my cousin, K-Man."

"What's good?" Dro nodded as he stepped in the house.

"Where D-Man?" Nore asked.

"In the back. D-Man, come up front! We got company!" K-Man called. "Y'all chill. Y'all want somethin' to drink? Got some brews and shit."

"Gimme a brew," Nore said, going for a PlayStation joystick.

"Y'all good?" he asked Dro and Mariana.

"Give us some brews, too," Dro said, accepting the southern hospitality.

When K-Man left the living room, his identical twin walked in. "What it do, cuz?" D-Man grinned, showing off gold teeth.

"You got it. This Dro and Mariana. He the plug."

Surprise and excitement shone in the twin's eyes. "What's hangin', brah? I seen you somewhere before. Where you from?"

"I'm not from round here. I'm from Milwaukee."

D-Man's eyes grew wide. "Oh, shit! You the nigga that fucked up PJ at the club!"

Mariana and Nore gave him surprised looks.

"That nigga threw a drink on me 'cause I was talking to his girl. I'm a gangsta. I ain't no bitch."

D-Man busted out laughing.

"What's funny?" K-Man asked as he handed out beers.

"This the nigga that fucked up PJ."

K-Man's eyes grew wide. "Oh shit! That was you?"

Dro was already tired of talking about the incident. "Yeah. It is what it is. Pussy niggas get fucked when they run across a nigga that don't fuck around. What y'all think about that work?"

The twins got to the money.

"That shit is some flake, mane. We need to talk numbers," K-Man said.

"That's what I'm here for. I need to get rid of this shit and get the fuck out the A. How much can y'all move?"

"Slow bidness right now 'cause this ain't our lane." D-Man spoke up. "But we making a way. That shit got niggas talkin' and it's about to pick up. How much of that shit you got?"

Dro wasn't going to let him know that much information. "Enough. Y'all bought twenty grams a couple times. What you think you can do with fifty? I know the shit lethal. Y'all can hit it and double it. Just Gimme five G's."

"That shit sounds like we finna get a bag!" K-Man smiled. "As long as you got that shit, we gon' move that shit."

"Cool. I'ma go through y'all. Keep my name out this shit. I'm tryna fly low and get the fuck outta here without making no more noise."

"We got you, brah. Fuck them pussy-ass Duffle Bag Bitches. I neva like them niggas n-e-way." D-Man laughed.

***

Dro sat at the table scooping white powder from the bag and putting it onto a scale. When the digital number got to fifty, he put the powder in a separate bag and tied it.

"How much longer do you think it will take to sell it all?" Mariana asked as she watched from the bed.

"I don't know. It took a week to sell forty grams. They said people hearing about the work and wanna buy. Just gotta wait and see."

"Do you trust them?"

He gave her a look. "Hell nah. I don't know them niggas."

"How do you know they won't betray you?"

"I don't. But if they do, I'ma be on they ass. And the one thing I don't do is fuck around."

She smiled. "Good and bad."

"Nah. Just serious," he said before looking down at the phone vibrating on the table. An unknown Milwaukee number showed on the screen. He thought about not answering. Only a handful of people had his new number and he didn't recognize the one on the screen.

"Hello?"

"Hey, nephew. You as hard to reach as the president," Crush joked.

"What up, Unc? You out?" Dro asked, happy to hear his uncle's voice, but hoping they weren't on a jail call.

"Yeah. I got bail earlier. Been tryna find you. Had to make a lot of calls."

"Whose phone you on?"

"I just bought it from the gas station. One of them disposable ones. I'ma throw away the SIM card as soon as we done talking. You okay?"

Dro looked around the hotel room. "I'm a'ight. Landed on my feet and found some fortune. Had a situation at the club. Fucked around and got into it with one of the biggest names in the city. I handled it. Tryna move on before they catch up with me. What about you? What happened with the charge?"

"It's still pending. They got my DNA on that envelope. That's all they got. All circumstantial evidence. They really want you. And now that them pigs got fried, they really eager. I talked to the district attorney, twice. They think you did it. And you made the news for Shamika, Isis, and that nigga. They talked to most, if not all, of the family. They really looking for you."

"I knew this was gon' happen. I'm not surprised. I'm ahead of 'em, though. I tried to disappear, but these fuck niggas, Duffle Bag Boyz, got in my way. All over a bitch. And I tried to walk away. Nigga threw a drink at me when I turned by back. So I beat his ass. But I did catch a blessing. Once I finish working it, I'ma move again."

"Damn, nephew. I wish I could help you out, but I got my own troubles. I just wanted to let you know what was going on this way. I won't make a habit of calling you. Only when it's important."

"Yeah. I appreciate the heads up. If you need to, you can tell 'em I did it. I might be cooked, Unc. If they catch up with me, I'm done. I'm not letting 'em take me to jail and lock me in a cell for the rest of my life. One more body on me won't matter if it will get you off."

"We not about to have that discussion, nephew. I don't do no tellin', even if I didn't do it. I'm not getting up on the stand and testifying against nobody. Especially you."

"I told you I'm not going to court. Ain't no sense in risking yo'self getting taken away from yo' girls again."

Crush was silent for a moment longer than necessary. "We will figure it out. Take care of yourself, baby boy."

"I will. You too."

Mariana was staring in his face when he looked up.

"Who was that?"

"My uncle. That trouble back home getting serious."

"You are wanted by the police?"

He nodded. "Yeah. And I ain't letting 'em take me to jail. You sure you wanna take this ride with me?"

"Yes. I don't have anyone else. Plus, I feel safe with you. I like that you are good and bad."

He stared in her eyes for a moment. The young Latin woman was growing on him by the moment. She lay on the bed in a feminine pose, the green sundress pooling around her like a fabric puddle. They had been sleeping on opposite sides of the same bed. He'd thought about sex with her almost every night, but couldn't make a move. Knowing that she was someone's sex toy didn't sit right with him. And he thought she might be scarred because of the experience.

"Better be careful. Sounds like you like getting in trouble and I might be too much."

Danger and lust shone in her brown eyes. "I am a grown woman. I know how to handle myself in any situation. I know when to be good and when to be bad."

The look in her eyes, her accent, and the way her lips formed the words, had Dro ready to fuck. "You think you bad as me?"

She met and held his stare. "I'm badder."

"Show me."

She got up from the bed and pulled her dress off in one motion. Beneath it she wore a black bra and panty set. She had a healthy frame, somewhere between skinny and thick. A handful of titties. A nice little tight ass. She walked up to Dro, bending to kiss him.

"Hold up, shorty!" He pulled away.

She looked surprised. "You don't want to do it?"

"Yeah. But I don't kiss."

She read him like a book. "Why? Because I was Manny's girl?"

"Yeah. I don't know what you was doing. Let's just do what we do."

"Let's not." She mugged him. "I am not a nasty girl. I had regular doctor visits before I came to America. And Manny had his doctor check me. I don't have disease, punta. I don't think you're a dirty nigger like everyone says about black people."

Dro stood and snatched her by the arm. "You betta watch yo' mouth!"

Her bad side was starting to show. She faced him, poking her chest out. "Or what? You going to rape me? They say all black men like to rape. You like to make girls cry and take advantage, don't you?"

Dro didn't know how to respond. She was giving him crazy eyes. Almost like she was challenging him. The atmosphere was charged and highly sexual. So he went with the flow and kissed her. Mariana released all of the bad girl, letting out wild moans as she turned the kiss very aggressive. She started biting his lips.

"Hold up!" He pushed her away, checking for blood.

She giggled, eyes turning to sexy slits. "Did I hurt you?"

Dro accepted her challenge and began stripping. "You wanna do this? Let me show you how real niggas get down."

She watched in excitement, turned on by his anger and aggressive energy. When he snatched off his underwear, her eyes popped.

"Bring yo' ass here!" he said, grabbing her by the throat and throwing her on the bed. "Open yo' mouth."

She allowed him to manhandle her, opening wide, one of his hands still wrapped around her throat. He shoved his dick in her mouth, making her gag. Then he began punishing her tonsils. Her eyes bucked as she gagged and lurched like she was about to hurl, spit coming from her mouth and nose. When he realized she couldn't swallow him and was about to throw up, he slowed his aggression, only giving her half the pipe. Relief shone in her eyes as she hung in there. Dro continued to fuck her mouth. Not having pussy in a week had him close to the edge. Instead of allowing her to taste his seed, he ripped her bra, freeing her breasts. Right when he was about to bust, he snatched out and shot off on her chest and face. Mariana moaned in ecstasy, sticking out her tongue to catch a drop. She loved the show and wanted more. Dro didn't disappoint. He grabbed her by the hair, taking her over to the table and forcing her to lay on her back. He grabbed her panties and ripped at them roughly. Mariana had to hold onto the table or be thrown on the floor. When the panties were off, he rolled her onto her side, lifting one of her legs. Before him was all pussy. Clean shaved. Swollen pink lips shining with juice. She started speaking in Spanish when he shoved his dick inside.

"Oh, shit!" Dro groaned. Mariana had a shot. It was tight, wet, and warm. When they were pelvis to pelvis, he paused, looking her in the face while letting her walls adjust. She looked high, eyes low and red, like she was having a good time. He gave a grin before moving his hips slowly. He pulled all the way out, giving slow half strokes and watching his dick disappear into her pretty pussy.

"Ah, Dios mios! Do it harder!" Mariana sang.

The Spanish was music to Dro's ears, making him go faster. He held her in place and long stroked, slapping his pelvis bone against her pussy every time he thrust forward. Mariana went crazy. She thrashed around on the table, slapping the wood and screaming. Her orgasm was so loud that he thought about stopping.

But he didn't. He flipped her onto her stomach and drilled her from the back. Mariana's ass cheeks were turning red from the way he beat it up. When he felt his nut, the thought to pull out of her crossed his mind. But he didn't listen. Instead he plunged deep inside and let his seed go swimming.

J-Blunt

CHAPTER 16

Dro stood in front of the safe, unable to take his eyes off the money. Four hundred thousand dollars. Cash. A brown rubber band was wrapped around each ten thousand dollar stack. It was beautiful, and it was all his. Well, most of it. Mariana had gone from sidekick to his bitch. What was hers was his. It took a month to move five hundred grams. He still had four and a half birdies to fly. The bag that he was taking when he left the A could have a few million dollars. He never imagined being able to say that. Now it was a few months away.

"What you gon' do with the money?" Whisper asked.

They were in the Black House. The twelve foot safe was bolted to the floor of the wine cellar.

"I don't even know, man. I can't start a business. Nigga name too hot for that. Unless I can get new papers. Unc, tell me you know somebody that make fake identities."

Whisper closed the safe, a thoughtful look on his face. "I might know somebody. Shit, I don't know why I didn't think to call this nigga sooner. If I was you, I would get a new identity and get the fuck outta the States. Try to get yo' way to one of them islands. Puerto Rico or somethin'. They won't never stop looking for you for all the shit you connected to."

Dro gave the words some thought. "That might not be a bad idea. I can live good over there with a couple mil."

"The cost of living is cheap. And yo' girl speaks Spanish so you won't be too far out of touch."

He thought about Mariana. She wanted to stay in America, enjoy the life she'd seen on TV. "Yeah, that might take some work. I think she caught up in the hype of being in America."

Whisper laughed. "She's a bitch, young Dro. She follows you. The one with the plan. Not the other way around. You all she got. You call the shots."

Dro nodded, appreciating the lesson in pimpology. "I'ma figure something out, man. I think I need to get a house and get the fuck out this hotel. I'ma probably be here for a while. Can you plug me on that, too?"

"Yeah. You know I got you. I'ma introduce you to the agent that found this for me. She'll clean the money for you, too. I got you."

"Good lookin' out, Whisper. I don't know what the fuck I would do without you."

When his phone rang, Dro looked down at the screen. It was K-Man. "What up, my nigga?"

"You know you got it, boss. I need another flip."

"A'ight. You at the crib?"

"Nope. But I can meet you there."

"Do that. I'ma grab it and come to you." After ending the call, Dro turned to Whisper. "A'ight, pimpin'. I gotta catch a check. Keep my shit safe. I'ma come back and get it."

"You know I got you. This Fort Knox. Ain't nobody comin' in the Black House and taking shit."

From the mansion, Dro went to the hotel to get K-Man another fifty gram pack. As soon as he walked in the door, Mariana was on him.

"Where you been? Why did you leave me in the hotel all day?"

He walked to the closet and grabbed the shoebox with the dope in it. "I told you I had something to do. You can't come everywhere with me."

"Why not? I am not your girl?"

Dro sat on the bed. "Look, Mariana, I like you. And I like what we do. But you not my girlfriend and I ain't yo' boyfriend."

Her face reflected the pain caused by his words. "But we had sex. I only sleep with my boyfriend. I am not a prostitute."

"I didn't say you was. But I'm not yo' boyfriend. Let's just do us and get this money. Don't complicate shit by doing too much. We good where we at. Just friends."

An angry fire passed through her brown eyes. "You think you will treat me like Manny? Use me and then throw me out?"

"Nah. You trippin'. You good. We good. Look, I didn't wanna tell you this, but I got a girl. I love her. And she about to have my son. I can't be with you like you want. That ain't for us."

She slapped the dope out of his hand, some of it spilling onto the floor.

"You got drugs and money because of me! I should be girlfriend. You fuck me last night."

Dro stood and shoved her. "Ay, man! Watch out! Don't be slappin' nothin' out my muthafuckin' hand. What the fuck wrong wit'chu? We ain't finna be on this crazy shit. You betta calm yo' ass down."

Mariana went loco. She started waving her arms and cursing in Spanish. "Oh, you wanna call me crazy! I show you crazy. Watch this."

She grabbed the shoe box. One hundred fifty grams inside. Dro didn't hesitate. No way she was about to fuck up thousands of dollars' worth of dope. He grabbed the box and tackled her to the ground. She fought back, scratching him on the face. He reached an arm back and slapped the shit out of her.

"Calm yo' ass down, bitch!"

Mariana froze, grabbing hold of her left cheek. Her eyes were spaced out, like she had taken a drug. He got up slowly, wondering what the fuck he got himself involved in when he gave her the first ride. This bitch was way too crazy. He picked up the bag that she slapped out of his hand. A little bit of the drugs spilled out, but most of it was still there.

"I'm sorry," she apologized, remaining on the floor, holding her face.

Dro just stared at her, unsure how to respond. She had gone from zero to one hundred and back to zero in less than thirty seconds.

She crawled to her knees. "I didn't mean to make you mad. I think something is wrong with me. I am good and bad. I told you."

Understatement!

"Listen, Mariana. I don't know what to say to you, but I can't be yo' man. And I'm not about to be fighting you. This ain't me."

She crawled over to him, wrapping herself around his leg like a child. "I am sorry. Please, don't be mad. Please, forgive me."

"Okay. A'ight. Let me go. Get off me."

"First, you say you forgive me. I'm sorry."

"A'ight. I forgive you. Let me go."

She unwrapped herself from his leg and started unbuttoning his pants. "Let me make you feel better. I will show how sorry."

Sorry head from Mariana turned out to be sloppy toppy. She used lots of spit and made fuck noises as she slurped on his tool. When he busted, she swallowed it all. He began zipping his pants.

"A'ight. I gotta make a drop."

"I am coming." She smiled.

***

"I think you should get a house and get the fuck out that hotel, my nigga. We gettin' it. Shit got these clucks and dope boys goin' crazy. You gotta be somewhere ducked," K-Man said.

Dro couldn't see the look on his nigga's face because he was focused on the TV screen. A Fortnite mission had most of his attention. "I hear you, my nigga. I'm looking into it right now. I really don't wanna be here that long, but this money so good that I can't leave. I really ain't no hustla. I used to jack niggas. But I do love the dope money. It comes fast."

"If you do leave, at least gimme the plug."

"I don't got no plug. I stumbled across this shit."

K-Man looked offended. "C'mon, my nigga. You ain't gotta lie to me. Just say you don't fuck wit me like that."

Dro glanced at him quickly before turning his focus back to the game. "I'm not bullshitting. I hit a lick for that shit. When I run out, I'm done."

"You serious?"

"Yeah, my nigga. I ain't lyin'."

"Damn. You need to find out where it came from 'cause we can get rich on this shit. They want it. If you can set it up, me and bro can run shit. You can be in the background runnin' it up."

Dro nodded. "I got enough of this shit to get us rich. Trust me. Just focus on saving y'all paper."

K-Man's phone rang. He answered on speaker.

"Nore! What up, sucka-ass nigga?"

"Them bitch-ass niggas robbed us and shot yo' brother!"

K-Man's smile was replaced with a mug. "What you say? What you talkin 'bout?"

"Trice and Richie Rich. They robbed us and shot D-Man. I'm driving to the hospital right now. Hold on, brah. We almost there."

K-Man shot to his feet. "Where them bitch-ass niggas at? I'm killin' them pussy-ass fuck niggas."

"They caught us down on Peachtree. I don't know where they at. They was talkin' 'bout us stepping on they toes and fuckin' up they money."

That got Dro's attention. "Who is Rich and Trice? What they take?"

"Bitch-ass Duffle Bag Boyz!" D-Man screamed in the background.

"They took thirty grams and a couple G's. Acted like they wanted to cop and upped on us. Caught us slippin'," Nore said.

"Brah, you good?" K-Man asked, on the verge of tears. "Where you hit at?"

"Fuck nigga hit me in the stomach and chest." He groaned.

"Nore, get my nigga to that hospital. I'ma be there later. Right now I'm finna go get them bitches."

After ending the call, K-Man grabbed his pistol and looked to Dro. "What you finna do?"

"Nah, what you finna do? Go to jail?"

K-Man raised his voice. "Them bitch-ass niggas just popped my brother. Fuck the police."

"I hear you. Them niggas took from me and shot yo' brother. They gon' get it. But we can't be stupid about it. We gettin' money now. Can't be moving without thinking. Let's do our homework. Hit these niggas hard and get away with it."

***

Today was a good day. Trice walked out of the car dealership smiling. He was dressed in Giuseppe. The sun was shining. Not a cloud in the sky. He had money in his pocket. A bad bitch on speed dial. And he was the owner of a brand spanking new money green Aston Martin Vanquish.

"I'm a boss!" Trice laughed as he climbed in the whip and pressed the start button.

From the dealership, the dope boy cruised through the city and flexed the new wheels. Everyone he passed gave approving stares and double takes. A few females looked like they wanted to fuck the car. The phone ringing made him look down. It was his nigga, Rich.

"What it do, fool?"

"Shit. Seein' what up wit'chu. Where you at?"

Trice hung an arm out the window as he pulled up to the stop light. The sunlight reflected off the diamonds in the Patek. "I'm out here flexin', my nigga. My Aston just came in and I'm out here fuckin' the city!"

"Oooh! Come get me right now, nigga! Let me see that mu'fucka!"

"I'm on my way. Where you at?"

"I'm by Shalisha's house."

"A'ight. I'm on my way."

Trice took the long way to Shalisha's house, soaking up more of the shine as he cruised through the city. When he pulled up to her house, he tapped the horn a couple times. Richie Rich came out smiling, long dreads swinging as he hopped up and down.

"Whoo! You fuckin' the game hard, my nigga. This what winning look like!"

Trice stepped from the car like he was walking on air. "You see me shining, bitch! And I iced out the Patek on these hoes. Watch out, li'l bitch! Saucy as fuck!"

After climbing back in the car, the Duffel Bag Boyz cruised the city. They drowned in the drip and rode the waves created by flossin'. They hit all the hot spots and made a scene everywhere they went, drawing the attention of players, haters, jackers, and killers. The Duffel Bag Boyz owned the city. Nobody came at them when they overstepped or were in the wrong. It was not a secret that the clique popped shit and left plenty of niggas in the morgue. They had no worries. No cares. So when the black Jeep began following, they didn't even notice.

"Pull over right here. Let's get these hoes," Rich said, pointing to a group of women standing on the bus stop.

Trice turned up his nose. "Nigga, I ain't fuckin' wit' them basic-ass bus stop hoes."

"Nah. Look. Them two bad!"

Trice followed his nigga's finger. Two females stood on the bus stop looking way flyer than all those around. Light skin. Tight revealing clothes. Heels on their feet.

"Oh, hell yeah!" Trice smiled, pulling up to the bus stop. "Ay, y'all need a ride?"

One of the basic women gave a gap-toothed smile. "Hell yeah!"

Richie Rich mugged her. "Not you. Fall yo' weak ass back. Ay, shawty with the long braids. What up with you and yo' girl? Y'all wanna ride wit' the Duffel Bag Boyz?"

"'Bout time we met some real niggas. Duffel Bag Boyz! Yeah, we need a ride."

Richie Rich hopped out to let the women in the backseat. "My name is Richie Rich and this my nigga, Trice."

"I'm Shamara and this my bitch Nikki. You gettin' in the back seat wit' me. right?" she asked, looking Rich up and down.

He checked her out. Long braids, cute face, full lips shining with gloss. She wore a halter top, tight skirt, and heels. Although she was the skinny one, she looked the best.

"Yeah, I'm gettin' back here. What you thought?"

When the women climbed in the car, the stunting and flexing continued. They stopped to get drinks and something to roll up before continuing the party on wheels. When Shamara ducked in the seat, it caught Trice's eye. Through the rearview mirror, he could see Richie Rich's eyes close as the woman's head began bobbing.

"Yeah, nigga! Get it!" Trice cheered. "Ay, Nikki. I'm tryna get down too. What up? Fuck with yo' boy."

"Pull over, baby. I got you. But I don't do nothing for free." She smiled.

"You ain't said shit. What you want? A bag?"

Trice found the nearest alley and pulled in. Before he could get the car in park, Nikki was undoing his zipper. When her mouth touched his dick head, he knew it was about to be crackin'. After adjusting the seat, he got comfortable, ready to enjoy the head. He had just got into it when the sound of screeching tires made him look up. A black Jeep had pulled alongside the foreign whip. A nigga climbed out dressed in black, holding an AK-47. Trice looked in K-Man's face and froze. He knew he was about to die before the bullets started flying.

Brrrrreaaaaatttt!

***

Dro sat back, his arms resting on top of the booth head rests. He looked out over the strip club. A party was in full effect in Roxan's. According to K-Man, the joint was underrated, but had some of the baddest bitches in the A. And he wasn't lying. Dro had been to many strip clubs, and Roxan's had some of the best looking dancers he'd ever seen.

"Make that shit clap, baby! Make it clap!" Nore cheered as he showered a dancer with money while she twerked.

"Get, get, get it!" K-Man joined in, slapping her jiggling booty cheeks.

"This is amazing," Mariana slurred. "I am having so much fun."

"This what you like, huh? Strip clubs and naked women." Dro laughed.

"No. It is the experience. The sexuality. It feels freeing. The women are beautiful and have nice bodies."

Dro agreed with her. "Yeah, they do."

"I like her."

Dro followed Mariana's finger. She pointed to a thick fair-skinned woman with purple hair. She looked mixed race or Latin.

"Shit, I like her, too."

She slapped him on the arm. "Dro! No."

"What? I was talkin' 'bout getting a lap dance. Want me to call her over?"

"Ooh, yes!"

Dro stood, waving his arms and getting her attention. "Ayy! C'mere! Come join our party."

She didn't hesitate. She knew they had money and walked over wearing a smile. There were bottles of liquor and stacks of money on the table. She knew this was where the party was at.

"What's up, baby? What can Kylie do for you?" she asked, striking a pose, hand on hip.

"What up, Kylie? My girl feeling you." Dro said. "Show her a good time. This her first time in a strip club."

Mischief shone in the stripper's eyes as she walked over to Mariana. "Hey, baby. This your first time?"

Mariana nodded. "Yes. You are sexy. Will you dance for me?"

"You the one that's sexy. I will do anything you want, cutie."

"Turn up then, Mariana!" Nore cheered, loving the girl on girl action.

"Ay, Dro. You think about what I said about staying?" K-Man asked.

"Yeah. I do like it here and the money good."

The twin smiled. "Hell yeah. I fuck wit'chu, my nigga. You a real nigga and a goon. And we gon' have the Duffle Bag bitch asses moved around. It's a takeover!"

"It's a takeover!" Dro cheered.

"We need a clique name, dawg. Ay, Nore. We need a clique name."

Nore took his eyes off the dancers to join in the convo. "Hell yeah. We should be BBB. Big Bag Boyz."

K-Man bust out laughing. "Hell nah! That shit weak as fuck."

"Keep it simple," Dro spoke up. "Young Rich Niggas. Like them ASAP niggas. I'm Young Rich Nigga Dro. You Young Rich Nigga K-Man. Young Rich Nigga Nore."

K-Man and Nore smiled approvingly.

"Yeah that's it. Young Rich Niggas in the building!" K-Man screamed.

Dro hoisted a bottle of Aces in the air as his phone rang. It was Twenty.

"What it do, my Savage nigga?"

"Ruben?" a female questioned.

"Who is this?" He frowned.

"Damn. This Lana. I know it's been a li'l while, but I hope you didn't forget me."

A warm feeling flooded Dro's chest as he remembered the last time he'd seen Lana. "Hey, baby. You know I didn't forget about my favorite cursing Christian."

"Hey, man. Where you at? The club? Yo' background is loud as hell."

He stood and walked to the bathroom. "I'm in a strip club. Hold on. I'm going to the bathroom. What's up? How you been?"

"I'm okay. Um, I don't know if you know this, but you been in the news."

"Yeah. I heard about that," he said, not offering any information or explanation.

"Twenty didn't wanna give me your number so I made him call you. I just wanted to let you know that regardless of what they say, I still think you a good nigga. I didn't know you was involved in the street like this. But I guess I shoulda knew because you is Twenty's so-called brother and he bad as hell."

"I ain't that bad." He laughed. "Just misunderstood. But I appreciate you calling. I thought about you but I couldn't reach out to you. I got some issues, you know?"

"That's an understatement, nigga. I'ma let you get back to the party. Just know that I'm here if you ever want to talk. And if you ever do step back in Milwaukee, make sure you come see me."

"Okay. I'ma do that. Take care of yo'self."

"You too."

CHAPTER 17

"Jimmie Anderson?" Dro questioned as he looked at the ID and Social Security card.

"That will get you past most minor police interactions. Traffic stops and whatnot. But it ain't good enough to pass Customs and the more serious checks," Katon explained. He was a false identity expert. He made a living stealing identities and making up fake ones.

Dro handed him the envelope with twenty-five hundred dollars inside. "A'ight, man. Good looking. I might need another one soon."

"You got the number. Hit me up," Katon said getting up from the table and leaving the restaurant.

"Let me see." Mariana said, snatching the ID. "Ooh, you look so cute, Jimmie!"

"Fuck you." He laughed.

Her eyes squinted to sexy slits. "Ay, papi. Don't tease me. Take me home and fuck me. I want to be a sexy nurse today."

Dro eyed his girl for a moment. Mariana was crazy, but he liked her. And she was a straight-up freak. Wanted to fuck all day. Loved to roleplay.

"You ain't said nothin'. But I don't want a nurse. I want you to be a naughty nurse!"

They left the soul food restaurant and hopped in the black Cadillac SRX. The drive to their new house in Gwinnett County took twenty minutes. It was a custom-built two-story brick house with columned porticos. Two bathrooms, four bedrooms, two fireplaces, and a two-and-a-half car garage. The price tag was three hundred thousand dollars.

When they walked in the house, Mariana raced to the master bedroom to get dressed. Dro went to the kitchen to grab the bottle of Hennessey. He was closing the refrigerator door when his phone rang. It was an unknown Milwaukee number. He got a tingling in his gut as he answered.

"Hello?"

"Hey, nephew. What up?" Crush greeted.

"Just got back from getting my new ID and shit. I'm Jimmie now," he cracked. "What's up with you?"

"I'm good. Taking it one day at a time. The fact that you ain't jumping off the wall right now means you haven't heard."

The hint of good news made Dro's heart rate increase. "Heard what?"

"You a new daddy, man! Forever had the baby."

Dro almost dropped the bottle of liquor. The words took a moment to register. And when they did, an indescribable excitement filled his being. "Oh shit! You serious? When you find out?"

"Your mother called Candice about an hour ago and told her. I didn't know if they had your number, so I called. Don't worry. This another one of those disposable phones. I'ma get rid of it soon as I hang up."

"Get rid of it now 'cause I gotta go. I gotta call Forever." Dro's hands shook as he dialed her number. He hadn't talked to her in two months. His son was here. He wished he could've been there for the birth. She answered on the third ring.

"Hello?"

"Hey, baby. It's me. I heard you had the baby."

"Ruben! Hey, baby!" she cried. "I've been trying to find you. Ruben Jr. is so beautiful. He looks just like you."

Dro got emotional, tears filing his eyes. "Damn, baby. I wish I coulda been there. When did you have him? How big is he?"

"Last night. He is big. Eight pounds, nine ounces. It took four hours for him to come out. He's laying next to me asleep. Hit me on Facetime so you can see him."

Dro called her right back. She answered with wild hair, like she had been in a fight or had a bout of wild sex.

"You look tired, but still beautiful."

"Aw, thank you!" she melted, turning the phone to their new born. He slept on her chest wearing a blue onesie with a matching hat. Ruben Jr. had light skin and looked almost white. Seeing his son made Dro's chest hurt. He wished he could be there to hold him.

"Man, that's a handsome li'l dude."

"All the hospital staff said that. Your mom and dad are coming to North Dakota to see him."

"That's good. I'ma try to get to you soon. I wanna see him too."

Fear shone in her eyes. "No. Don't come. The U.S. Marshals came and talked to me. They are looking for you."

He let out an angry breath. "Damn. I knew that shit was gon' happen. What did they say?"

"They searched the house and threatened to take me to jail if I didn't tell them where you were."

"That's why I couldn't tell you where I am. I knew they would try that."

"I seen you on the news too. And I looked online. You are in a lot of trouble. Three murders. What are you gonna do, baby?"

"I don't know yet. Stay hiding. I'm doing good where I'm at. I —"

"Dro, where are you?" Mariana called, walking into the kitchen. "What are you doing, papi? Why didn't you come upstairs?"

Dro was caught off guard. He had gotten so caught up in his son being born that he forgot to be careful about Mariana and Forever. And now it was too late.

"I'm on the phone. Gimme a minute."

"Who is that?" Forever asked, getting an attitude.

"C'mon, papi! I need you now!" Mariana begged, pulling his arm. She didn't care that he was on the phone or who he was talking to. She wanted to fuck.

"Chill! Stop!" he said, his face serious. "Go ahead. This an important call. I'ma be up in a minute."

Mariana's demeanor changed from freaky to feisty. "What do you mean? Who you talking to?"

"Ruben, who is that? Is that a woman?" Forever asked.

Dro left the kitchen and walked towards the back door. "Look, Forever, baby, that ain't nothin'."

Forever looked hurt. "Are you sleeping with her?"

"C'mon, baby. Let's not do this right now. You just had the baby."

"No! We're doing his right now. You have a woman telling you to come on. Are you about to have sex with her?"

Dro stepped into the backyard, trying to decide what to say. He was caught. Lying would make it worse. "Her name's Mariana. She lives with me. I don't love her and she not my girl. I love you and I told her that. She knows about you and the baby."

Devastation spread across Forever's face, tears spilling from her eyes. "Why, Ruben? I just had your baby and you go and cheat on me? I told you I would wait for you. Why couldn't you wait for me?"

He ran a hand across his face in frustration. "I don't know. 'Cause I'm a man. I need pussy. She don't mean nothing to me. It's just sex."

Forever wasn't hearing it. "Just sex? What do you mean, just sex? That doesn't make it okay. Sex is everything. You're living with and having sex with somebody that isn't me. How can you say you love me if you're cheating on me and hurting me?"

"C'mon, baby. I told you she - "

Forever disconnected the call, not letting him finish talking.

"Fuck!" he cursed, leaning against the house and closing his eyes.

"I don't mean nothing to you?" Mariana hissed.

Dro opened his eyes and saw her stepping outside. Anger blazing in her brown eyes.

"C'mon, now. We ain't finna do this."

"No. We doing this. You wouldn't have nothing without me. I got you drugs and money, but you say I mean nothing? You are the one that is nothing. You are a coward. You - "

Dro moved quickly, grabbing her by the face and squeezing. "You betta watch yo' mouth, bitch! You wouldn't be shit without me. I saved yo' ass. Manny threw yo' ass out like trash. Yo' ass wanted to die. You would be dead if it wasn't for me. I'm the one getting the money. I'm the one taking care of you. Don't you ever disrespect me again!" he snapped, shoving her into the side of the house before walking inside.

Mariana snapped. She chased behind Dro and punched him in the back of the head. The blow wasn't hard, but being hit and the stress of arguing with both women was enough to set him off. He dropped the phone and spun around, back hand slapping Mariana in the face. She fell to the floor. He climbed on top, wrapping both hands around her neck.

"Bitch! I told yo' punk ass not to fuck with me!" he cursed, squeezing as hard as he could.

Mariana's eyes bulged, veins popping out all over her face and neck. She grabbed at his hands to stop him from choking her. It was no use. He was too mad and too strong. The whites of her eyes turned red, her face pale blue. Death was moments away.

And then his phone rang. The sound of the phone vibrating on the hardwood floor got his attention, pulling him from the point of no return. Figuring it might be Forever calling back, he let go of Mariana's throat. She gasped and choked, sucking in deep gulps of air while he checked the caller. It was D-Man.

"What up?" he answered, out of breath.

"Dro, it's all bad, my nigga. Nore just got popped by Twelve."

Devastation washed over him. It was all becoming too much. "Fuck. What happened?"

"I don't know exactly what happened. The li'l thotty he was wit' called me and said he got flagged tryna make a move. They caught him with some work and a heat."

Dro shook his head. "A'ight. I'ma find him a lawyer and get that bail money. If you talk to that nigga, make sure you tell him not to call me. I'm too hot to be taking a jail call. But tell him I'ma get him out and get him a lawyer."

"Fa sho', my nigga. He know how it go. I'ma holla at his sister and tell her to find out what that bail is. I'ma get at you when I know somethin."

"A'ight."

Dro threw the phone down and sat heavily on the couch. Three problems had punched him in the face in a matter of minutes. Forever was mad. Mariana lay on the floor struggling to catch he breath. And his li'l nigga was locked up. Damn. He needed some air and time to think of his next move. So he went outside and hopped in the Cadillac SRX. During the drive, he called his nigga.

"Dro, what it do, nigga?" Luna answered.

"It's all bad, my nigga. Where you at? I need to holla."

"I'm at the Black House. 'Bout to get ready for this black tie event. What's good?"

"I'm on my way. I'ma holla when I get there."

"Damn, my nigga. You sound fucked up. Come through. Stay dangerous."

"You know it. Savage."

Dro pulled up to the Black House and was let in by Prianka.

"Hey, Dro. How you been?" She smiled.

He let out a heavy breath. "I'm tryna figure it out. Where Luna?"

"Upstairs in the great room."

Dro climbed the stairs and found his boy standing in front of six dime pieces, giving a speech. He stopped at the door to listen.

"Check it out. We gon' go in here and get this cash. Don't be fuckin' around. These niggas got money. They looking for classy in public, but nasty behind doors. Let's stay focused. A'ight? No bull-shit tonight."

"Damn, My nigga. You in here sounding like a real pimp."

Lunatic spun around and saw Dro smiling.

"Ay, y'all go get ready. We leavin' in a couple minutes," Luna told the women. "What up with you, my nigga? I'm just in here givin' a last minute pep talk. Come in. Chill and roll up. What got you stressing?"

When the women left, Dro took a seat on the couch. After grabbing some weed from the pile on the table and a wrap, he talked. "Forever had the baby. Li'l nigga handsome as a mu'fucka."

"That's what's up, nigga! Why you trippin' on that? That's good news."

"I ain't tripping on that. I'm trippin' 'cause Forever found out about Mariana. She got mad. Then Mariana heard me tellin' Forever that she wasn't shit so she got mad and hit me. I damn near killed that bitch. Choked her until she damn near passed out. Then, while

158

I'm choking her ass, D-Man call me and tell me Nore got knocked wit' some work and a pistol."

Lunatic shook his head. "Damn, my nigga. When it rains, it pours."

"I know. I'm gettin' tired of Mariana and I need to find Nore a lawyer. Where Whisper?"

"I don't know. Call that nigga. You need to get Nore straight so he can know you really fuck with him. Niggas nowadays don't believe in that keepin' it gangsta shit. Especially if they think niggas left them on stuck."

"Yeah, I'ma get him right. I'ma call Whisper when I leave. I gotta figure out what to do wit' Mariana's crazy ass, too. Bitch loves drama, my nigga. She wanna fight and fuck every day."

Lunatic laughed. "That's that Spanish blood. You know them Latina hoes be crazy. Wanna cut niggas n-shit. But she did get yo pockets right. That shit should be easy to fix. Go fuck that bitch and put her in check. You ain't gon' be able to stop her from being crazy. You just gotta figure out if you wanna deal with it. Might have to learn how to play her games so you can be ready. Get a step ahead of her. Beat her to the argument. You gotta take that power so you can control the relationship."

Dro gave his nigga a look. "Damn. That shit was on point. You sound like a li'l Hoe Whisperer."

"My nigga, I'm cold with this pimp shit. Don't no bitch stand a chance against me. I'ma pimp in my own fuckin' mind!"

After leaving the Black House, Dro hopped in the Cadillac and called Whisper.

"Young Dro! What's up, nephew? I was just thinking about calling you."

"What's good, man? One of my niggas got knocked and I need to get him a lawyer. You know somebody?"

"Yeah. You know I got you. I'ma have my man call you. He specializes in all that street nigga shit. But on some other shit, I need you to listen. This shit is real. I just got word that Manny and his people got a picture of you and yo' dame hittin' that house. They had cameras. They don't know who you is, but they askin' around. Might be time for you to find a new city."

Dro played Lunatic's words in his head. When it rains, it pours.

"A'ight. I'ma keep my eyes open and try to figure something out soon."

"Young'un, you gotta take this one serious. This not the Duffle Bag Boyz. This a cartel, and they got unlimited money and reach. Stay outta sight."

"A'ight. I'ma take it serious. I just need to get that lawyer so I can straighten out my li'l nigga. I don't need this nigga thinkin' I forgot about him and doin' no fuck shit."

"You got it. I'ma get on that as soon as we hang up."

***

Dro drove home with a lot on his mind. The cartel had his picture. Damn. He didn't remember seeing any cameras in the house. They must've been hidden. But why they had cameras and no alarms was a question he couldn't answer. Maybe because there were drugs inside and they didn't want the alarms to bring the police. In any event, he was taking the situation seriously. He would have to put Atlanta in the rearview mirror soon.

And then there was Mariana. She was a head case. But the advice from Luna was on point. He planned on going home and fucking her like she wanted and making up. Starting tomorrow, he would create his own fights with her to keep her in line. Shit was crazy, but he had to stay ahead of her and run the relationship.

When he walked in the house, Mariana sprang from the couch, wrapping him in a hug and kissing him. She still wore the nurse outfit. On her neck were large bruises left from his hands choking her.

"Aye, papi! I am sorry. Please, forgive me," she pleaded, her voice hoarse and scratchy.

"Okay. Let me go."

"No. First say you forgive me. I am sorry, papi."

"A'ight. I forgive you. But we need to talk."

160

She released him, wearing the smile of a woman that had just gotten her way. "Okay. But we talk later. For now I want to make love. Come to the room. Please."

Dro allowed Mariana to lead him up the stairs. When they got to the bedroom, she took control, kissing him while taking off his clothes. After he was naked, she pushed him onto the bed and began kissing him all over. When she got to his dick, she sucked him into her mouth slowly, taking her time. Dro closed his eyes and enjoyed her mouth. When the sucking stopped, his eyes shot open. Mariana was crawling up his body. After positioning herself, she grabbed his dick and sat down on it. She rode him slowly, kissing his chest and neck. Dro's hands found her ass cheeks and he closed his eyes again, enjoying the ride.

He didn't notice Mariana's hand slipping under the pillow, grabbing the Glock. She moved slowly, watching his fuck face. When the gun was firmly in her hand, she stopped riding and sat up. Dro opened his eyes just in time to see her point the gun in his face. Then everything slowed down. He could see the murderous look in her eyes. She held the gun with both hands, applying pressure on the trigger. She was about to kill him. Instead of laying down and dying, he moved his head to the side while simultaneously bucking his hips and going for the pistol.

Pop!

The gun fired. Dro could feel the heat from the bullet as it whizzed by his face. He flipped Mariana over, taking the 40 from her and pinning her to the bed by her throat. In her eyes he could see the fear and regret. But that wasn't enough to stop the judgment. He touched the barrel to her forehead and squeezed the trigger.

Pop!

J-Blunt

CHAPTER 18

"Bitch-ass shit!" Dro cursed as he stared down at the dead body. He couldn't believe she tried to kill him. Mariana was crazy, no doubt. But he didn't think she was that crazy. Looking at her dead body made the decision to leave a no brainer. Atlanta was officially burnt up. He was out. After finding his phone, he called Whisper.

"I just got off the phone with my lawyer friend, Raymond. He should be calling you soon," Whisper answered.

"Fuck that lawyer, pimpin'. I need to get the fuck outta Atlanta. I need that money out the safe right now."

Whisper heard they urgency in his voice and got concerned. "What's goin' on, nephew? You good?"

"Nah, Unc. This bitch tried me and I fucked her up. I gotta go."

"What bitch? Yo' li'l flower?"

"Yeah. I don't wanna say no more. When you going home? I need to get that money and hit it."

"Damn, Dro. I'm a couple towns over. I'm wrapping up some business. I need a li'l more time. I can be at the Black House in 'bout two hours. Can you lay low 'til then?"

Dro didn't want to wait, but it seemed he didn't have a choice. "Yeah. Okay. I need to get rid of this trash anyway. I'ma get at you in a minute."

After hanging up, Dro stared down at her half-naked body. A lump had formed on her forehead where the bullet went in. Blood ran down her face. The sheet beneath her head was a bloody mess. He would have to get rid of the body and the whole mattress.

But there was no time for all that. He needed to get gone. The only result was to set the house on fire. Hopefully it would burn long enough to destroy all the evidence of Mariana's body and him ever being in the house.

After packing some clothes, his guns, and the three and a half kilos of heroin, he searched the bathroom and found a bottle of rubbing alcohol. He emptied it on her body and the bed then lit the flame. The fire quickly ignited, engulfing the entire bed in flames.

He grabbed the bag, ran outside and jumped in the SRX. He called D-Man as he drove.

"What's good, my nigga?"

"Where you at?" Dro demanded.

"Out makin' a move. What's poppin'?"

"Fuck that move. I need you to meet me at yo' house. It's an emergency."

"Okay, okay. Say no more. I'm turning around right now. I'm like ten minutes away."

Dro drove carefully towards the twin's house, watching the mirrors and obeying all traffic laws. The last thing he needed was to be pulled over. He was stopped at a red light when the gas gauge caught his eye. The Cadillac was damn near on E. He reluctantly stopped at the gas station to get some petro. While he was pumping gas, a black Lincoln Navigator pulled up to the pump across from him. Mariachi music played from the SUV's speakers. Three middle-aged Latino men climbed from the truck. The driver remained behind the wheel.

Dro was watching the meter on the gas gauge when he felt eyes on him. It was the Navigator driver. After making eye contact, the driver looked away. An eerie feeling crept into the Savage's gut. Instead of second guessing, he stopped pumping the gas and put the pump back up on the base. While he was locking the gas cap on the Cadillac, one of the Latinos came from the gas station and climbed in the truck. Dro was walking around to get in the rental car when he noticed the driver point at him. Not wanting to test fate, he climbed in the truck and got the fuck out of there. During the drive he kept the 40 on his lap and watched the rearview mirror.

Ten minutes later, he pulled behind D-Man's Grand Prix and sent a text. A few moments later the twin came out, his gold teeth shining as he approached the truck.

"What's hangin', mane?" he asked, hanging his head in the window.

Dro reached in the suitcase and pulled out 450 grams of diesel. "I gotta ride out, brah. This for the squad. I got love for you niggas and I didn't wanna leave y'all fucked up. Make sure you bail Nore out and get him a lawyer. Don't be on no fuck shit."

D-Man took the work. "I got you brah. I ain't no fuck nigga. I'm a real nigga. But why you leavin all of a sudden? What happened?"

Dro eyed the twin, wondering how much he should tell him. "I had to off my bitch. She tried to do me in."

D-Man's eyes popped. "You bullshitting?"

He shook his head. "Nah. She really tried me. I burnt shit up. I gotta - "

Tires screeching made Dro look over. The black Navigator pulled to a stop alongside of the Cadillac. Two pistols hung out the front and rear passenger windows.

Pop, pop, pop, pop, pop, pop, pop, pop, pop!

D-Man hesitated, moving too slowly. A bullet hit him in the face. Dro ducked low in the seat, slamming the car into drive and smashing the gas. D-Man's body flew a couple of feet as the Lac shot forward. It only went a few feet before slamming into the back of the Grand Prix. Without hesitating, he put the car in reverse and hung the 40 out the window, clapping back at the Latinos as he zipped past the SUV in reverse. When the Cadillac was clear of the Navigator, he yanked the steering wheel. The Cadillac's tires screamed as the SRX spun around. Then he hit it in drive and smashed the gas. The engine revved as the Cadillac picked up speed.

Dro watched in the rearview as the Navi did a U-turn and sped after him. Bullets clanked into the body of the rental car as a high-speed shoot out ensued. Dro kept his head low, swerving through traffic, dodging cars and hoping the police didn't get involved. He was speeding down a residential block when a pink Ford Focus pulled out of a driveway. The gap between the Ford and the car parked on the other side of the street was small. Dro knew he couldn't stop. The cartel members would gun him down if he did. Instead of breaking, he smashed the gas and attempted the tight squeeze. The Cadillac barely made it through the tight space, clipping the Focus' bumper and making the car spin. The Navigator was going too fast to avoid the collision. Dro watched in the rearview mirror as the Lincoln smacked the pink sedan. There was a loud crash, and metal and fiberglass exploding in all directions.

Dro breathed a sigh of relief. The chase was over. And not wanting to take the hot car to Whisper's house, he parked a few blocks over, grabbed his duffel bag, and beat his feet. During the walk, he wrestled with what to do next and where to go. He was all out of options and choices. He looked to the sky and thought about praying. He decided to save his breath. He had experienced bad fortune ever since he had come to Atlanta. God had obviously turned His back. Twenty's words about being his own god passed through his head. Dro would have to be his own god. When he got to the Black House, he waited on the front porch until the white Rolls Royce pulled into the driveway. Whisper climbed from the car and immediately noticed the look on Dro's face.

"You okay?"

"Hell, nah! I just ran into them cartel niggas. They tried to get me, man. I barely got away. I think they fucked over my li'l nigga D-Man."

Whisper looked around. "Where they at? Did they follow you?"

"Nah. They crashed. Everybody in the truck might be dead too 'cause we was going fast."

"Damn, nephew. It's time for you to go. Come on in and get yo' money. What happened with you and the li'l Mexican dame?" Whisper asked as they walked on the house.

"Bitch tried to shoot me in the face while we was fucking."

Whisper looked surprised. "Say what?"

"Yeah. She heard me talking to Forever. Heard me say she didn't mean shit to me and hit me. I damn near choked her to death. Then I get the call that Nore got knocked and that shit was too much. I came and holla'd at Luna and he tellin' me to get on her level and control the relationship. So I go back and fuck her, ready to play her game. While the bitch riding me, she pulls out a pistol and tries to shoot me. I offed her and set the whole house on fire."

Whisper paused on the stairs, eyeing Dro in amazement. "Damn, young Dro. Yo' life is crazy, baby boy. But, at least you got a nice piece of change and a new identity. Think about what I said. Puerto Rico ain't a bad place to start over at."

***

"How you wanna play this, Coupe?" Dirty asked as he put out the blunt.

"Let me do the talking. I'ma tell him I wanna seat at the table. If he ain't tryna hear it, we on to plan B."

Dirty smiled. "I like plan B."

"I really don't wanna go there. I been knew this nigga since I was a pup. I hope he listens and feels me."

"I like plan B, too," Bam-Bam spoke up from the back seat of the Benz truck. "We can squad up and do our own shit. Find a good plug and drop the numbers like yo' brotha had it. We can take all the action. Niggas in the street loyal to gettin money."

Coupe laughed. "You think you know yo' shit, huh, li'l nigga?"

"I'm just stating the obvious." Bam-Bam shrugged.

Dirty looked back. "You gon be a cold li'l nigga. Make sure you stay close and listen."

After climbing from the Benz, the trio walked in the auto detailing shop and headed for the back office. Trill was sitting behind the desk smoking a Cuban cigar, talking in the phone. Two of his shooters sat close. When Coupe and his shooters walked in the office, Trill put up a finger, signaling them to hold on. After finishing the call, he addressed the men.

"What's good, my niggas? Coupe, you was talking like the situation was life or death. What's the emergency?"

"I wanted to holla about the business. I think I should have my brother's spot."

Trill leaned back in the chair, a smirk spreading across his face. "What is you talking about, man? Where this coming from?"

"I'm talking about me getting Monster's slot. I been hearing rumblings about how you moving and shaking. Er'body ain't on the same page. I think I can help settle niggas down. They expected me to take my brother's spot after he got killed, but I wasn't ready. Now I am."

Trill laughed. "Okay. I hear you. Monster been dead for a minute now. Where is all this coming from?"

"I feel like it's my time. I been out there moving and shaking. Niggas respect me. They know I'm one hunnit and I do niggas right."

Trill nodded, remaining silent for a couple moments. Then he leaned forward, his elbows on the desktop. "Check this out, Coupe. You know I fuck wit'chu. You like my li'l brother. But you didn't help start this and this ain't no democracy. It was me and Monster grinding that put food on the table for the team. You wasn't a part of that, and you don't get to inherit a spot just because yo' brotha had it."

"But er'body ain't on the same page. Niggas grumbling."

"And they can do that grumbling shit all they want. I got control of most of the defense on the North side. I set the prices. If niggas don't like it, they can move around. I'm tryna eat, not win popularity contests."

Coupe felt the sting in the words. "So it's like that?"

Trill kept strong eye contact. "Yeah, brah. I told you I ain't makin' room for nobody. You didn't help build this. If you wanna get money, let's do it. But I ain't about to play politics. I think I heard you out long enough. If you was anybody else, I'da been cut this conversation short."

Coupe searched the drug leader's face for a sign of weakness or unsureness. There was none. "I guess you said it all."

"So how you wanna play it? Is we gettin' money or what?"

Coupe nodded. "Yeah. We gettin' money. I just wanted you to hear me out, and you did that."

Trill got up and walked from behind the desk with open arms. "I hope it ain't no love lost. I gotta be firm when it comes to business."

"It's all good, brah. You know it's all love," Coupe said as the men shared an embrace.

CHAPTER 19

Dro climbed off the Greyhound bus, gripping the duffle bag tightly. He made it out of Atlanta. It felt like a minor miracle. He had gotten into so much shit that he didn't think he would make it out alive. Almost lost his life several times. But somehow, by the grace of God, he made it.

And now he was back where it all started. Milwaukee was cold. The winter had come roaring in, freezing everything. Snow covered the ground. Thanksgiving was a week away. And as bad as he wanted to stay to be with the family, he couldn't. It wasn't safe for them or him. He had come to Milwaukee for one reason, one really stupid reason that he hoped he wouldn't regret. After getting an Uber, he settled in the back seat and took the nervous ride. Twenty minutes later, they reached the destination.

"Here you are, buddy," the driver said, parking at the curb.

Dro handed him a fifty. "Keep the change."

"Hey, thanks man! That's real cool." The white man smiled.

Dro left the car, thankful that it was dark outside. He was taking a big risk by coming to the Mil, but felt good operating in the night. It would be harder for someone to identify him. After walking upon the porch, he rang the doorbell. A few moments, later a female answered.

"Who is it?"

"Ruben," he answered, opening the screen door.

Locks clicked and the door swung open. Lana's pretty face came into view. Seeing the blonde hair and juicy lips made him smile. She wore a T-shirt and leggings. Her eyes reflected the surprise at seeing him.

"Hey, baby! I didn't - "

His lips upon hers took the words away. Lana kissed him back for a moment. When his hands got too frisky, she pulled back.

"Wait, baby! Hold on."

"Dayum, sis! I see you." Bianca smiled. "Hey, Dro." She waved.

"Sup, Bianca?" He nodded before stepping in the house. "My bad. I didn't know you had company."

Bianca got up from the couch to give him a hug. "Uh-uh. I ain't gon' be here too much longer. It look like y'all got something to do."

"Shut up! I hate you," Lana teased before turning to Dro. "Come in. Sit down. Why didn't you tell me you was coming?"

He gave her a look. "You know I couldn't do that."

She immediately realized her mistake. "Right. Right. I don't know what the hell I was thinking."

"You bad as fuck, Dro," Bianca spoke up, shaking her head. "You was all over the news, nigga. The reward on yo' ass is a hundred thousand dollars. Bet' not let nobody see you. I don't even know why you came back to Milwaukee. I know my sister pussy ain't that good."

Lana smacked her lips. "Shit! You betta tell her, baby."

"I'm finna go away for a while. Ain't no telling the next time I'ma be able to see some of my people. I just wanted to holla one last time."

"You turning yo'self in?" Lana asked.

He frowned. "Hell nah. They gotta catch me. But I'm going where don't nobody know me. And I'm leaving as soon as possible. I just wanted to see you before I left."

Lana turned to her sister. "I love you, but it's time for you to go. He don't got that much time."

Bianca faked an attitude. "Damn, bitch! I told you I was finna leave. Don't rush me. Bye, Dro. Fuck her in the ass since she talking shit. And make her bleed."

When Bianca left, Lana locked the door and spun to him. They stared at each other for a moment before she hugged him.

"Man, I missed you so much, Ruben. It's crazy because I barely know you. And you dangerous. But I want you so fucking bad."

"That's because I can hit them deep spots," he joked.

She pushed him playfully. "Stop playing!"

"Nah, but seriously. I missed you, too. That's why I'm in Milwaukee. The whole bus ride I questioned what the fuck I was doing. But I had to see you one last time."

She stared up into his face for a few moments, searching for the truth behind his words. After finding what she was looking for, she reached up to kiss him. Their lip lock was wild and full of unbridled passion. Hands roamed bodies like they had minds of their own. Moans of desire filled the living room as they made their way to the couch. They paused long enough for Dro to drop the duffle bag and undress. Lana watched him, shedding her own leggings and T-shirt. When they were naked, she sat on the couch. He walked in front of her, his dick pointing at her like a big-ass finger. Lana grabbed hold of him and opened wide.

"Damn!" Dro moaned, closing his eyes.

Lana sucked him slowly, only able to get a little of him in her mouth. Her head game needed work, but she could do enough to get a man off. She used her hand to stroke what she couldn't get down her throat. Dro liked what she was doing and right when he thought it couldn't get any better, she moved her mouth to his sack and began sucking his balls while continuing to jack him off. She sucked each one individually before taking them both in her mouth and humming. The vibrations from her throat sent a shock through his body. After giving his balls some attention, she went back to sucking him. Dro's toes began curling as the nut came gushing out of his dick like a geyser. Lana kept her hand pumping, catching his nut in her mouth, but not swallowing.

"Aw shit!" he groaned.

After he was drained, she reached for the cup on the table and spit in it. Before she could move a muscle, Dro dropped down to his knees, spread her legs, and attacked her pussy. He used his fingers to spread her lips apart and lick her clit.

"Oh, yeah! Baby, yeah!" Lana moaned, rubbing the back of his head.

When he put his lips around her pearl tongue and began sucking, Lana went ham. She started winding her hips and smashing his face against her pussy. And when he slipped two fingers inside her, it drove her crazier. Her orgasm came rushing out like a tsunami.

"Oh, shit! Oh, Ruben! Aaaahhhh!"

After her orgasm passed, Dro wiped the cum from his lips and spread her legs wide like a pair of scissors. His dick slipped easily into her wet pussy. He didn't wait for her to adjust. It was too good.

He began fucking her hard, her big titties bouncing wildly as he held onto her thighs and drilled away.

"Yeah! Oh, yeah! Ssss, Mmmhhh!" she moaned.

The sound of her pleasure was music to his ears. It was invigorating, made him want to go harder. And he did. He fucked her until her legs were shaking. Then he flipped her over and went in her ass. He slapped her big-ass booty while digging deep into her colon. Her asshole was tight and Lana went wild, loving everything he was doing. When he felt his nut coming, he pulled out and busted on her back.

Lana spun around and kissed him. "I hope you don't think we done. I don't know when I'ma see you again. Let's go take a shower."

After a round of sex all over the bathroom and a shower, they retired to the bedroom to kick it and smoke. About thirty minutes into their relaxing, the doorbell rang.

"You expecting somebody?" Dro asked, getting nervous. He had left his pistol, dope, and money in the duffle bag on the living room floor. Thoughts of Bianca calling the police to collect the reward also crept into his head.

Lana checked the time on her phone. It was 9:17. "That might be my mama dropping off Alana," she said before throwing on a robe and leaving the room.

Dro crept to the bedroom door and listened.

"Who is it?" Lana called

He couldn't hear the person outside but he clearly heard Lana's response.

"Boy, what do you want?"

Dro searched the closet and found another robe. A nigga was coming in the house and he wasn't about to leave six hundred thousand dollars and three kilos of heroin unattended. Plus, his pistol was in the bag. After finding a fluffy bright yellow robe, he threw it on and stepped out the room. There was a tall light-skinned young nigga standing in the living room. When he saw Dro, he looked down at Lana, smiling.

"Oh shit! You got company?"

172

"Yes. Now what do you want, Brian?"

He laughed. "Chill, girl. I just need somewhere to chill for a minute. My nigga finna ride down on me," he explained before turning to Dro. "What up, playa?"

"Sup, brah?" Dro nodded, going for the duffle bag and his clothes. After gathering his things, he spun and headed back to the room.

"Who is yo' friend you got coming to my house?" Lana asked.

"My nigga Dirty. Who is yo' friend?"

Hearing the name made Dro pause at the bedroom door. The hairs on the back of his neck stood up and a fire burned within him. He spun around, thinking fast. He couldn't let Lana say his nickname. He also wanted to play it cool and not show any aggression.

"My name Ruben. What's good? Who is you?"

"I'm Bam-Bam. Her li'l brother."

Dro walked over and extended a hand. "What's good, li'l bro? You smoke?"

"Hell yeah!" The youngster smiled.

"I got some loud from Atlanta in the room. Lana, you wanna grab that?" Dro asked.

She smacked her lips and rolled her eyes. "He not finna stay here."

"He said he waiting on his nigga. I just wanna show yo' li'l bro some love," Dro said.

Lana stomped towards the room while the men had seats.

"Yo' sister be trippin sometimes, huh?" Dro laughed, tossing the duffle bag on the couch.

"Hell, yeah. Be tryna treat me like I'm still five. A nigga out here thuggin' and tryna get a bag."

"I can love that," Dro agreed. "What you out there moving? I might be able to get you a plug."

"You not finna talk to my li'l brother about selling drugs," Lana cut in, coming out of the room with the weed and a wrap.

"He grown, baby. Chill. Let me kick it wit' li'l bro."

She rolled her eyes. "Whatever."

"Yeah, Ruben. Check her ass!" Bam-Bam laughed.

"It ain't too late for me to kick you out," Lana mugged.

"Chill, sis. I'm just fuckin wit'chu. But yeah, brah, if you know a plug on that H, that would be live."

Dro wanted to celebrate, but he kept his composure. "Oh yeah! My man got plenty of that shit."

Bam-Bam smiled like he just got the best news. "On what?"

"That's my word. Look, gimme yo number and I'ma hit you and let you know what his numbers is. I probably need like a day 'cause he outta town. Went to the Chi to get fresh."

Bam-Bam laughed. "Man, me and my niggas need this. That's crazy. They say God works in mysterious ways."

Dro smiled. "Amen."

After kicking it with Bam-Bam and smoking a blunt, the youngster's ride showed up. Dro thought about following her little brother outside and giving it to Dirty. But that meant he would have to kill Bam-Bam, and probably Lana. That would be too messy. So he bided his time. Besides, he had something they wanted.

"Let me see yo' phone," Dro said.

"It's in the room. You ready for another round?" She winked.

"Yeah. Let me make a call real quick. Can you grab me something to drink?"

She got up from the couch and walked towards the kitchen. "I got you, baby. Hydration is important when you working out."

While she was in the kitchen, Dro ran to the room to make the call.

"Twenty, where you at, nigga?"

"At the crib. What up wit'chu?"

"I'm on my way over. You ain't gon believe this shit."

"What? You in Milwaukee?"

"Yeah. At Lana's house. I'm finna have her drop me off. Stay dangerous."

"That's all I know. Savage."

***

"What up, Unc?" Dro smiled, wrapping Crush in a strong hug.

"It's good seeing you, nephew. But you know you shouldn't be here."

"I know, man. I just had to see you one last time. I'm about to leave for Puerto Rico and I'm not coming back. Plus, I was able to find Dirty. Killing two birds with one stone is worth the risk."

"Yeah. I hear you. So, what y'all need me to do? Do I need me to get my gun dirty?"

"Nah," Twenty spoke up. "We got that. We just need you to pull up and create the diversion. We got it."

Dro nodded. "Yeah, man. You did enough for me. You don't gotta put in no more work. You retired now. Worry about that case. What is Brandon saying?"

"Same ole thang. They can't put me at the scene. They just saying I gave the money. The DA knows you did it. They just want me to snitch."

"I told you to tell them I did it and get yo'self off. Ain't no sense in you going to jail for nothing," Dro reasoned.

"That ain't the point, nephew. We family. Ride or die. Real niggas do real thangs. I'ma take my weight. They gon' do what they gon' do."

"That's real shit." Twenty nodded.

"Well, if you change yo' mind, you know what to do."

Twenty mugged Dro. "Quit tryna get Unc to snitch, nigga. He keepin' it one hunnit. I love to see gangsta shit. Don't try to turn Crush into one of these fuck niggas. He ridin' it out."

Dro laughed. "Yeah. A'ight. Look, Unc. I'ma text these niggas and tell 'em to meet us by the school on Courtland. All you gotta do is pull up. When you hear the shots, drive off. A'ight?"

"Okay, nephew. You know I got you. Stay dangerous."

Twenty and Dro gave the old timer a look.

"Man, y'all betta quit looking at me like that. I know I ain't a part of the clique, but I'ma savage too."

"You got it, Unc." Dro laughed. "Stay dangerous."

The old timer smiled. "That's all I know how to do. Savage love."

***

"Look for a green Regal." Coupe said as he turned the Benz truck onto 36th and Courtland.

"There it go. By the school." Dirty pointed, gripping the Mac-11 as he looked around. Something didn't feel right about the meeting, and he was on full alert. They had stumbled upon the plug too easily. And the buyer, a nigga named Crush, said he could get bricks for sixty thousand. Most things that sounded too good to be true were just that. Too good to be true.

"Y'all watch my ass. Dirty, get out with me. Bam-Bam, keep that chopper ready," Coupe said as he parked the truck behind the car.

"Y'all act like this a buy. Ain't y'all just finna talk numbers?" Bam-Bam asked, not understanding the extra precautions.

"Sixty a brick for some untouched sounds too good to be true," Dirty said.

"I think he good. I told y'all my sister fuck wit' the nigga. We good."

"Yeah. We gon' see," Dirty said, concealing the Mac under his sweater as he reached for the door handle.

Before he could open it, the Regal pulled away. Dirty's instincts kicked in and he drew the Mac.

Twenty ran from behind the school building, the AK-47 spitting fire as fast as he could squeeze the trigger. Dro was close behind, squeezing off two 40s with extended thirty round clips. Coupe was caught off guard. He had just stepped out of the truck when the shooting started. The chopper bullets hit him in the chest, knocking him into the side of the SUV. He fell in the street, wounded but still alive.

Bam-Bam was also caught off guard by the sudden shooting and froze. He wasn't trained for war, and that was his mistake. High-powered rounds punched through the SUV's frame and tinted windows, gravely wounded the youngster.

Dirty moved quickly, opening the door and jumping out of the Benz. He took cover and listened to Bam-Bam's screams as slugs tore into the truck's frame. He peeked his head out and saw the Savages running towards the truck, their guns blazing. Knowing he was outmanned and outgunned, he refused to be a sitting duck. Dirty lifted the Mac-11, firing wild shots as he retreated behind a garage.

The Savages reached the Benz at the same time. Dro pointed the 40s at Coupe, finishing him off with bullets to the face. Twenty aimed the chopper at the truck's tinted windows and fired, making sure that whoever was inside wouldn't live to see tomorrow. After ducking wild shots from Dirty's Mac, the goons chased.

Dirty ran into the alley, glancing back every couple of feet to see if he was being chased. Dro came around the corner first. Dirty let the Mac ride, almost knocking him out of the game. The Savage ducked behind a garbage can just in time, the bullets slamming into the garage. Twenty came around the corner next and let the chopper ride. Several slugs caught Dirty in the back, sending him face diving into the snow. He rolled over and saw Dro and Twenty jogging towards him. Not wanting to go out by himself, Dirty grabbed the Mac-11. Dro let the 40s ride a couple times. The bullets caught Dirty in the chest, making him drop the gun. Then, just for good measure, the Savages stood over him and let him have it.

J-Blunt

CHAPTER 20

The ride to Spencer's house was nerve-wracking. So much had happened since the last time Dro spoke to Forever. He wasn't even sure she would let him in the house. But he had to make an attempt to see her and his son. As usual, he over-tipped the gracious Uber driver before climbing from the car. The walk up the walkway and onto the porch felt like a death row inmate's walk to the gas chamber. He knew he was about to go through a hard time. After ringing the doorbell, he waited. Didn't have to wait long.

"Who is it?" Forever called.

"It's me."

The locks clicked and the door opened. Forever's face showed mixed emotions. She was still pissed to find out about Mariana, but happy that he was still alive and free. Instead of a warm greeting, she left the door open and walked away.

"Forever, we not gon' talk?" he asked, following her into the house and locking the door.

She spun around, anger blazing in her pretty brown eyes. "About what, Ruben? You cheated on me!"

"I know. And I'm sorry that I hurt you. I know you won't like my explanation, but I'm a man, babe. She didn't mean nothin' to me. It was just sex."

"Just sex! Just sex?" She exploded. "Sex is everything, Ruben! You stuck your dick inside another woman. You expect me to be okay with that because it was just sex? You cheated on me. You had sex with somebody that wasn't me. We talked about marriage. We have a son. I love you. But you hurt me."

When the tears began spilling, Dro felt like a scumbag. He reached out, wanting to hold her. "I'm sorry, baby."

She slapped his hand away. "Don't touch me!"

He kept his distance. "I don't wanna fight you, Forever. I came to apologize and see my son."

She crossed her arms and mugged him before turning and walking towards the bedroom.

Ruben Jr was sleeping in a bassinet beside the bed. When Dro saw his baby boy, tears welled up in his eyes, heart swelling inside his chest. The one-week-old baby was wrapped in a blue blanket. He almost looked white. Dro dropped the duffle bag and reached down to pick him up.

"Stop! You're going to wake him up."

"I know. I want him to see me and hear my voice. I don't know when I'ma be able to see him again."

Forever softened, remaining standing with her arms crossed over chest and watched.

"Hey, li'l man. Wake up for Daddy. Lil Ruben, you beautiful, man," he cooed, taking a seat on the bed.

Small cries escaped the baby's lips as he woke up.

"Hey, hey. Don't cry, li'l man. Daddy just wanted to say hi. Hey, baby boy."

After a little more fussing, he opened his eyes and began staring at Dro.

"Yeah. That's it. Don't cry. Daddy is here. Hey, man. I want you to know that I love you. I might not be around while you growing up, but don't ever stop believing in my love."

Forever stood near, tears spilling down her face. The father/son moment had touched her deeply, stirring her emotions.

"Where are you staying?"

"I was in Atlanta, but I burnt it up. I'm about to leave the country. I'm in so much shit, baby. I gotta go. I just wanted to see y'all one last time."

"What happened in Atlanta?"

He looked up from his son. "Everything. And I was trying to chill, but it seems like trouble just finds me. I thought I was like Job, you know? I thought the hard times was temporary. But they not. Struggle is my life. Trouble follows me around like my shadow."

"I don't even know what to say. So much has happened to you. But I've been praying for you. It seems like it's the only thing I can do."

He nodded. "Yeah. I know. I'm sorry for bringing all this shit into yo' life. Last year, if somebody would've told me I would be running all across the States getting chased by drama and the police, I woulda called them a lie. I thought God had a plan for my life. I thought he was gon' use me to do big things. I guess that preacher was wrong."

Forever moved to sit next to him. "Just because you're in trouble don't mean that God can't use you. God is God. Our ways are not His ways. You just have to trust him. He has brought you this far. After everything you've, been through, you're still alive. That is something, isn't it?"

"I don't know. What good is being alive if you ain't free? I got a reward on my head and police chasing me."

"No matter if you're free or locked up, you will still be alive. That matters."

He shook his head. "No, it don't. And you sayin' that 'cause you never been locked up. I'm not going back to jail. Never."

"But the police are looking for you. What are you going to do?"

The truth shown in his eyes. Before he could respond verbally, the front door closing got their attention. Dro reached for the duffle bag.

"That's my dad," Forever said. "And he's mad at you."

Dro frowned. "Why?"

Before she could answer Spencer walked in the room smiling. When he saw Dro, that smile quickly changed into a frown.

"What the hell you doin' in my house, man?"

The tone in Spencer's voice caught him off guard. Ruben stood, unsure how to respond.

Forever jumped up to defend her baby daddy. "Daddy, he just came to see his son."

"I don't give a damn. You shouldn't have come here. Got the U.S. Marshals coming to search my house. They said you killed three people. I don't want you in my house or around my family."

Dro tried to keep his cool. "C'mon, Spencer. I ain't tryna argue with you, man. I just came to see li'l Ruben. They my family too."

"You don't give a damn about them. You almost got them killed. You don't think I know about the State Fair shit? That was because of you. You a danger to everybody you around. You already got yo' daughter killed and I'm not about to let you do that to my daughter and grandson."

Dro sat his son in the bassinet, anger flashing in his eyes. "Listen, man. You crossing a line. I told you I don't want no problems, but you not finna be talking to me like that."

Spencer didn't care about Dro's feelings or the flash of anger. "You crossed the line when you got my daughter shot. You crossed the line when you stepped in my house. I don't give a damn that you mad! I'm mad too. And you need to get the fuck outta my house. You not wanted here."

Dro thought about pulling a pistol from his duffle bag and blowing Spencer's brains out. But he loved Forever too much to cause her that kind of pain. So instead of killing her father, he tried to push him into a fight so he could beat his ass.

"Put me out, Spencer. Over there talkin' shit like you wanna try me. You ain't been around Forever her whole life. Don't make it seem like you a fuckin' daddy now. You a sperm donor, nigga. Fuck you, chump!"

Spencer became enraged and lunged at Dro. Forever grabbed her father, not wanting the men to fight.

"No, Daddy! No!"

"Let me go, baby! Let me go!" Spencer yelled, struggling to break away from Forever.

Dro blew him off and picked up the duffle bag. "Actin' like you struggling with yo' daughter is a joke, nigga. Chill. I know you know better than to try me. I'ma leave yo' house, but don't disrespect me no more. This the only time I'ma warn you."

Spencer stopped struggling with Forever, surprised that Dro had seen through the high capping. Not wanting another confrontation, he left the room, giving the family a moment.

Dro turned to Forever. "I'm sorry for everything, baby. I didn't want it to go down like this, but this is the way it is. I love you, for real. You got my whole heart. No matter what."

Forever abandoned her anger and gave in to the love. She wrapped him in an embrace, tears spilling down her face. "I love you, too. And I always will."

After sharing a kiss, Dro bent down to kiss his son. "I love you, man. Take care of your mother."

The baby stared up at him like he understood.

Leaving them was hard, but he knew it was time to go. Forever grabbed li'l Ruben and followed him from the room. Dro and Spencer exchanged mugs as he walked to the front door. After kissing the baby and Forever one more time, he opened the door. When he saw the police cars out front, his heart almost stopped.

He closed the door, pulling a pistol from his bag and pointing it in Spencer's face. "Yo' bitch ass called the police on me?"

"Ruben, no!" Forever screamed.

Spencer's hands flew in the air. "What? No, man! What police? I didn't call no police!"

"How the fuck they get outside then?"

Spencer looked out the window. "Shit! I don't know, Ruben. When I came home, they wasn't out there. I swear to God I didn't call them, man. Please. It wasn't me. I didn't even have time."

Dro looked to Forever. She held the baby tight, tears rolling down her face. "Please, baby. Don't shoot him. Please."

"Fuck!" Dro cursed. He looked out the window and saw the police organizing. They had armored cars, bulletproof vests, and a SWAT team. He ran to the back of the house and saw they had the house surrounded. There was no way out.

"Baby, it's over. You gotta turn yo'self in," Forever said.

Dro wasn't sure of his next move. But one thing was for sure: he wasn't turning himself in. "I can't let them take me. I can't go to jail for the rest of my life. I'm not spending the rest of my life in a cell."

Forever began to cry again. "But they won't let you get away. They have the house surrounded."

"I know," he mumbled.

"Ruben, you gotta give up," Spencer said. "Please, man. I don't want my daughter or grandson to get hurt."

Dro mugged him, still believing Spencer had called the police. "I'm not giving up. Fuck that."

"Daddy is right, baby. You have to give up or they might come in here."

Seeing the fear in Forever's eyes got to him. He had to make a decision. If the police ran in the house, they might shoot everybody. They were a black family in an all-white town. And they were harboring a murderer.

"Here. Take the bag. It's a half million dollars in here," he said, taking another pistol out.

Forever refused to take the duffle bag. "No. What are you about to do?"

Dro dropped the bag on the floor, tears forming in his eyes. He opened the door and saw the police pointing guns and hiding behind their cars. Then he turned to Forever. "Get away from the door. I love you."

"Wait, Ruben. Don't do this. Please!" she cried.

After one last look, he kicked the screen door open and ran outside, pistols blazing. In his head he recited the Lord's prayer, hoping that God would forgive him and have mercy on his soul.

The police didn't show him any mercy. They squeezed the triggers on their assault rifles until Dro was laying on the ground, no longer moving.

EPILOGUE

"A hungry person don't care what kinda silverware he eats with."

Drayez looked up from the book he was reading, eyeing his cellmate. "What you say, man?"

"God doesn't call us to be successful. He calls us to be faithful. When God calls you, He anoints you, or prepares you, for where He is gonna send you. It's not about where you are when He calls you, because when He calls you, you won't be ready. You won't be ready until you walk through the valley of the shadow of death. You won't be ready until you've been tried and tested. You won't be ready until you've gone through something," Ruben said, pausing to let his celly chew on the words.

"That was cold, Ruben," Drayez admitted. "Man, you sound like one of them TV preachers. What you doing in here? Why you ain't out there with yo' own church?"

Ruben looked down at the Bible sitting on his bed, gathering his thoughts. "I had my time out there. I wasn't always a Christian. I got two life sentences plus two hundred years. I seen a half mil in cash. Bricks of dope. Had sex with some of the finest women in the world. I shot so many people that I lost count. And all of that was my testing and trying. God allowed me to survive it all so I could come here and tell people the Good News. That God is real. Take this time and get right with God, man. Separation don't mean isolation from the world, but insulation."

Drayez looked at the pictures of Forever taped to the wall. She was the finest woman he had ever seen. "Do you regret anything? I mean, you sound like you was out there having yo' way."

Ruben looked to the picture of his son taped to the wall. Lil Ruben was the most handsome five-year-old the world had ever seen. "That's a hard question to answer, man," he said before taking off his shirt. Seven healed bullet wounds covered his chest and stomach. "I regret all of this. But what I learned is that when God asks you to do something, do it. If He's in it, he'll open doors for you. You'll know which ones to walk through. But whatever you do, don't try to take it all on your shoulders. Give it to God. His shoulders are bigger than ours. And where He guides, He provides. Always remember this, Drayez. Just like Daniel in the fiery furnace, heat reveals faith. When life starts to hit you, whatever is in you is what will come out of you."

Ruben ran a hand down his face. He wished that he could get a do-over with his life, but he refused to question God's plan. He knew that had he not lived THE SAVAGE LIFE, he would not have the testimony he now had. Yes, he would die in prison, but while he was alive, Ruben was going to spread the Word with the same fervor that he had once stomped the streets.

THE END

Submission Guideline

Submit the first three chapters of your completed manuscript to ldpsubmissions@gmail.com, subject line: Your book's title. The manuscript must be in a .doc file and sent as an attachment. Document should be in Times New Roman, double spaced and in size 12 font. Also, provide your synopsis and full contact information. If sending multiple submissions, they must each be in a separate email.

Have a story but no way to send it electronically? You can still submit to LDP/Ca$h Presents. Send in the first three chapters, written or typed, of your completed manuscript to:

LDP: Submissions Dept

Po Box 870494

Mesquite, Tx 75187

DO NOT send original manuscript. Must be a duplicate.

Provide your synopsis and a cover letter containing your full contact information.

Thanks for considering LDP and Ca$h Presents.

BOW DOWN TO MY GANGSTA

By **Ca$h**

TORN BETWEEN TWO

By **Coffee**

THE STREETS STAINED MY SOUL **II**

By **Marcellus Allen**

BLOOD OF A BOSS **VI**

SHADOWS OF THE GAME II

By **Askari**

LOYAL TO THE GAME **IV**

By **T.J. & Jelissa**

A DOPEBOY'S PRAYER **II**

By **Eddie "Wolf" Lee**

IF LOVING YOU IS WRONG... **III**

By **Jelissa**

TRUE SAVAGE **VII**

MIDNIGHT CARTEL II

DOPE BOY MAGIC III

By **Chris Green**

BLAST FOR ME **III**

DUFFLE BAG CARTEL **IV**

HEARTLESS GOON **IV**

A SAVAGE DOPEBOY II

By **Ghost**

A HUSTLER'S DECEIT III

KILL ZONE **II**

BAE BELONGS TO ME III

SOUL OF A MONSTER III

The Savage Life 3

By **Aryanna**

THE COST OF LOYALTY **III**

By **Kweli**

CHAINED TO THE STREETS II

By **J-Blunt**

KING OF NEW YORK V

COKE KINGS IV

BORN HEARTLESS IV

By **T.J. Edwards**

GORILLAZ IN THE BAY V

De'Kari

THE STREETS ARE CALLING II

Duquie Wilson

KINGPIN KILLAZ IV

STREET KINGS III

PAID IN BLOOD III

CARTEL KILLAZ IV

Hood Rich

SINS OF A HUSTLA II

ASAD

TRIGGADALE III

Elijah R. Freeman

KINGZ OF THE GAME V

Playa Ray

SLAUGHTER GANG IV

RUTHLESS HEART II

By Willie Slaughter

THE HEART OF A SAVAGE II

By Jibril Williams

FUK SHYT II

By Blakk Diamond

THE DOPEMAN'S BODYGAURD II

By Tranay Adams

TRAP GOD II

By Troublesome

YAYO III

A SHOOTER'S AMBITION II

By S. Allen

GHOST MOB

Stilloan Robinson

KINGPIN DREAMS II

By Paper Boi Rari

CREAM

By Yolanda Moore

SON OF A DOPE FIEND II

By Renta

FOREVER GANGSTA II

By Adrian Dulan

LOYALTY AIN'T PROMISED

By Keith Williams

THE PRICE YOU PAY FOR LOVE II

By Destiny Skai

THE LIFE OF A HOOD STAR

By Rashia Wilson

TOE TAGZ II

By Ah'Million

CONFESSIONS OF A GANGSTA II

By Nicholas Lock

PAID IN KARMA II

By **Meesha**

<u>Available Now</u>

RESTRAINING ORDER **I & II**
By **CA$H & Coffee**
LOVE KNOWS NO BOUNDARIES **I II & III**
By **Coffee**
RAISED AS A GOON I, II, III & IV
BRED BY THE SLUMS I, II, III
BLAST FOR ME I & II
ROTTEN TO THE CORE I II III
A BRONX TALE I, II, III
DUFFEL BAG CARTEL I II III
HEARTLESS GOON
A SAVAGE DOPEBOY
HEARTLESS GOON I II III
DRUG LORDS I II III
By **Ghost**
LAY IT DOWN **I & II**
LAST OF A DYING BREED
BLOOD STAINS OF A SHOTTA I & II III
By **Jamaica**
LOYAL TO THE GAME
LOYAL TO THE GAME II
LOYAL TO THE GAME III
LIFE OF SIN I, II III
By **TJ & Jelissa**
BLOODY COMMAS I & II
SKI MASK CARTEL I II & III
KING OF NEW YORK I II,III IV

J-Blunt

RISE TO POWER I II III

COKE KINGS I II III

BORN HEARTLESS I II III

By **T.J. Edwards**

IF LOVING HIM IS WRONG...I & II

LOVE ME EVEN WHEN IT HURTS I II III

By **Jelissa**

WHEN THE STREETS CLAP BACK I & II III

By **Jibril Williams**

A DISTINGUISHED THUG STOLE MY HEART I II & III

LOVE SHOULDN'T HURT I II III IV

RENEGADE BOYS I II III IV

PAID IN KARMA

By **Meesha**

A GANGSTER'S CODE I &, II III

A GANGSTER'S SYN I II III

THE SAVAGE LIFE I II III

CHAINED TO THE STREETS

By J-Blunt

PUSH IT TO THE LIMIT

By **Bre' Hayes**

BLOOD OF A BOSS **I, II, III, IV, V**

SHADOWS OF THE GAME

By **Askari**

THE STREETS BLEED MURDER **I, II & III**

THE HEART OF A GANGSTA I II& III

By **Jerry Jackson**

CUM FOR ME

CUM FOR ME 2

CUM FOR ME 3

CUM FOR ME 4

CUM FOR ME 5

An **LDP Erotica Collaboration**

BRIDE OF A HUSTLA **I II & II**

THE FETTI GIRLS **I, II& III**

CORRUPTED BY A GANGSTA I, II III, IV

BLINDED BY HIS LOVE

THE PRICE YOU PAY FOR LOVE

By **Destiny Skai**

WHEN A GOOD GIRL GOES BAD

By **Adrienne**

THE COST OF LOYALTY I II

By Kweli

A GANGSTER'S REVENGE **I II III & IV**

THE BOSS MAN'S DAUGHTERS

THE BOSS MAN'S DAUGHTERS II

THE BOSSMAN'S DAUGHTERS III

THE BOSSMAN'S DAUGHTERS IV

THE BOSS MAN'S DAUGHTERS **V**

A SAVAGE LOVE **I & II**

BAE BELONGS TO ME I II

A HUSTLER'S DECEIT I, II, III

WHAT BAD BITCHES DO I, II, III

SOUL OF A MONSTER I II

KILL ZONE

By **Aryanna**

A KINGPIN'S AMBITON

A KINGPIN'S AMBITION **II**

I MURDER FOR THE DOUGH

By **Ambitious**

TRUE SAVAGE

TRUE SAVAGE II

TRUE SAVAGE **III**

TRUE SAVAGE **IV**

TRUE SAVAGE **V**

TRUE SAVAGE **VI**

DOPE BOY MAGIC I, II

MIDNIGHT CARTEL

By **Chris Green**

A DOPEBOY'S PRAYER

By **Eddie "Wolf" Lee**

THE KING CARTEL **I, II & III**

By **Frank Gresham**

THESE NIGGAS AIN'T LOYAL **I, II & III**

By **Nikki Tee**

GANGSTA SHYT **I II &III**

By **CATO**

THE ULTIMATE BETRAYAL

By **Phoenix**

BOSS'N UP **I , II & III**

By **Royal Nicole**

I LOVE YOU TO DEATH

By Destiny J

I RIDE FOR MY HITTA

I STILL RIDE FOR MY HITTA

By **Misty Holt**

LOVE & CHASIN' PAPER

By **Qay Crockett**

TO DIE IN VAIN

SINS OF A HUSTLA

By **ASAD**
BROOKLYN HUSTLAZ
By **Boogsy Morina**
BROOKLYN ON LOCK I & II
By **Sonovia**
GANGSTA CITY
By **Teddy Duke**
A DRUG KING AND HIS DIAMOND I & II III
A DOPEMAN'S RICHES
HER MAN, MINE'S TOO I, II
CASH MONEY HO'S
By Nicole Goosby
TRAPHOUSE KING **I II & III**
KINGPIN KILLAZ I II III
STREET KINGS I II
PAID IN BLOOD **I II**
CARTEL KILLAZ I II III
By **Hood Rich**
LIPSTICK KILLAH **I, II, III**
CRIME OF PASSION I II & III
By **Mimi**
STEADY MOBBN' **I, II, III**
THE STREETS STAINED MY SOUL
By **Marcellus Allen**
WHO SHOT YA **I, II, III**
SON OF A DOPE FIEND
Renta
GORILLAZ IN THE BAY **I II III IV**
DE'KARI
TRIGGADALE I II

J-Blunt

Elijah R. Freeman
GOD BLESS THE TRAPPERS I, II, III
THESE SCANDALOUS STREETS I, II, III
FEAR MY GANGSTA I, II, III
THESE STREETS DON'T LOVE NOBODY I, II
BURY ME A G I, II, III, IV, V
A GANGSTA'S EMPIRE I, II, III, IV
THE DOPEMAN'S BODYGAURD
Tranay Adams
THE STREETS ARE CALLING
Duquie Wilson
MARRIED TO A BOSS... I II III
By Destiny Skai & Chris Green
KINGZ OF THE GAME I II III IV
Playa Ray
SLAUGHTER GANG I II III
RUTHLESS HEART
By Willie Slaughter
THE HEART OF A SAVAGE
By Jibril Williams
FUK SHYT
By Blakk Diamond
DON'T F#CK WITH MY HEART I II
By Linnea
ADDICTED TO THE DRAMA I II III
By Jamila
YAYO I II
A SHOOTER'S AMBITION
By S. Allen
TRAP GOD

196

By Troublesome

FOREVER GANGSTA

By Adrian Dulan

TOE TAGZ

By Ah'Million

KINGPIN DREAMS

By Paper Boi Rari

CONFESSIONS OF A GANGSTA

By Nicholas Lock

J-Blunt

BOOKS BY LDP'S CEO, CA$H

TRUST IN NO MAN
TRUST IN NO MAN 2
TRUST IN NO MAN 3
BONDED BY BLOOD
SHORTY GOT A THUG
THUGS CRY
THUGS CRY 2
THUGS CRY 3
TRUST NO BITCH
TRUST NO BITCH 2
TRUST NO BITCH 3
TIL MY CASKET DROPS
RESTRAINING ORDER
RESTRAINING ORDER 2
IN LOVE WITH A CONVICT

Coming Soon
BONDED BY BLOOD 2
BOW DOWN TO MY GANGSTA